3 Minutes and 53 Seconds

Branko Prlja

3 MINUTES AND 53 SECONDS

Translated from the Macedonian by Paul Filev

DALKEY ARCHIVE PRESS

McLean, IL / Dublin

Originally published by Goten as *3 minuti i 53 sekundi* in 2015.

Copyright © by Bert Stein (Branko Prlja), in 2015.

Illustrations copyright © by Branko Prlja, 2019.

Translation copyright © by Paul Filev, 2019.

First Dalkey Archive edition, 2019.

ISBN: 978-1-62897-350-1

Library of Congress Control Number:2019956387

Dalkey Archive Press

McLean, IL / Dublin

Co-funded by the
Creative Europe Programme
of the European Union

Printed on permanent/durable acid-free paper.

www.dalkeyarchive.com

Contents

3 Minutes and 53 Seconds

Branko Prlja

▶▶1984◀◀

"Thriller"—Michael Jackson

A DARK STAIRWELL made of large blocks of stone worn down over the years by the tread of thousands of students' feet, by the weight of their heavy thoughts and even heavier school-bags, almost as big as themselves. Back then it was called Silvije Strahimir Kranjčević Elementary School, but that was a mouth-ful and everyone called it simply SSK.

The playground asphalt was cracked from the tree roots pushing up from beneath. It was as if they were trying to break through the prison-like feel of the place, with its high wall. That wall was later to provide the backdrop to a sketch on a popular Bosnian comedy show called *Top Lista Nadrealista* (Surrealists' Billboard Chart). The famous sketch depicted a fight between garbage collectors from two different parts of the city, one from East Sarajevo, the other from West Sarajevo, in which they hurled trash at each other. It was as if a precursor of what was to come. Sarajevo became a divided city soon thereafter, but in a different, more sinister, more tragic way.

That school held many secrets, such as the secret of my gran-dad's fall down the stairs as he hurried to attend a parent-teacher meeting, the surgeries that followed, the blood clot, my depar-ture to Skopje, his telephone call from the hospital, his death, and his not having the chance to ask for my forgiveness . . . but all that happened later.

In 1984, Michael Jackson's "Thriller" was a big hit. My grandma and I were at home alone. She was ironing, I was watching TV, as the neighbors invited each other over for coffee by tapping on the radiator pipes. The music video started out innocently enough, but then got scarier and scarier. As if presaging what was to happen to him in the years to come, Michael Jackson's face was transformed into that of a monster, and I froze with fear. I hid my face in my grandma's lap. She was a strong woman who had endured war and deprivation, cold and rheumatism, diabetes, and years of waiting for her husband's release from the notorious Goli Otok prison camp for political prisoners. She filled me with not only admiration, but also a sense of security.

"What's wrong?" she asked in alarm, not waiting for my reply because she must have seen what was on the TV. "Now, now, don't be scared. It's just a film," she said, ruffling my hair.

I closed my eyes and turned my head away. The glow of the chandelier produced a yellow glare behind my eyelids. I could clearly see the sun above me, big and warm. I could hear the sound of the sea waves and the quiet, gentle breeze blowing through my hair . . .

When I opened my eyes she was no longer there. She had gone, leaving behind two men and a young boy with unresolved mutual issues, torn apart by divorce, quarrels, court cases, and even child abduction. I lived in fear, but not because of "Thriller" or *Nightmare on Elm Street*, a popular horror film at the time. They did scare me, of course. But what I was even more afraid of was the image of my mother that the people I lived with impressed on me, the people I loved dearly. In my mind and in my dreams, she was an evil witch chasing me, while I foolishly and desperately tried to get away from her, only to end up falling into a bottomless well, night after night. I would wake up screaming beside my grandad, who slept so soundly that nothing ever woke him.

Then I started seeing apparitions, things that didn't exist, and yet they were right there in front of me. Waking up always brought with it now and mysterious figures that I could almost touch before they simply vanished. I knew those figures wanted to tell me something, but I never worked out what it was because I didn't really give it much thought. When it comes down to it, kids want to live, not to think, especially when right outside your door something magical and unforgettable is taking place: the 1984 Sarajevo Winter Olympics.

One of the few childhood photographs that I still possess, and which didn't get lost in the whirlwind of the war, is a picture of me with Vučko, the mascot of the Olympic Games. But he was also something much more than just that. Vučko was a friendly image of a wolf. The wolf native to the forests of Yugoslavia, a proud and courageous animal that lives in a pack to which it owes its survival. Without the pack, he's just a lone wolf, doomed to live out his days waiting for the end, as we ourselves would soon end up doing.

"That's all now," the photographer said to me. "Come on, let go of Vučko. Other kids are waiting to have their photo taken with him." My grip on Vučko was firm. I didn't want to let go of him. I wanted him to be mine because he felt like something stable, something reliable, which I wanted to cling to. He was something positive and cheerful, something I could be happy about. And not only that, he brightened up everything at the kindergarten. The food they gave us there—the instant mashed potatoes that smelled like detergent, the macaroni cheese baked beyond recognition, the rice swimming in oil—the physical bullying by the older kids, the painful smacks of the teacher's ruler landing on my small hand, all of it seemed almost bearable because of him.

My grandma died. I saw my dad cry for the first time in my life. The second time would be six years later, when he said goodbye to me. The Winter Olympics came to an end. I became a first-grader. But none of that was important, since all my thoughts were of her alone—my first big crush.

►►1985◄◄

"We Are the World"—USA for Africa

I WAS EIGHT years old and Africa was in trouble. The world was mobilizing. At the helm, one of its biggest stars—Michael Jackson—led a chorus of other stars in the song "We Are the World." It was unforgettable. Anyone born in the late seventies remembers this as a magical moment, when the world came together to do something to help those less fortunate. Live Aid followed later. The West collectively laundered its conscience through music.

The images of malnourished black children with distended bellies and protruding ribs left a deep impression on us during childhood. We felt ashamed, guilty even, because we had enough food and water, we enjoyed free healthcare and free education, not to mention all the major amenities of life. But were we also "the world"?

The 1984 Winter Olympics ended and Yugoslavia finally earned its deserved place in the world, as the culmination of a dream—the dream of our Marshal Tito on a white horse, who led us to a brighter future. But he passed away, and the future began to look a lot less bright. After the Olympics, it was as if all our dreams had been shattered. And the germ that was to bring inflation, ethnic hatred, revanchism, and war began to sprout. The bobsled track, down which world champions once whizzed, became all but obscured by moss.

But none of us children sensed any of that. In the tradition of the Olympic Games, we continued to uphold the positive spirit of sport and unity. Each of us had a hockey stick, and we played with a tennis ball instead of a puck. We had a real blast.

The first snowfall of the season piled up high along our street, towering over our heads. In the morning we would go outside and plunge headlong into the snow. And later we spent the whole afternoon tirelessly, eagerly tamping it down.

One day, the team from the next street played against our street. The needlessly rough visitors physically dominated us on our home turf. One of our opponents was particularly aggressive. He tripped me up several times but I kept quiet. He was bigger, stronger, and more aggressive than me. And then he tripped me up again.

It was then that I remembered a story my dad had once told me. "I had just started at a new school," he said. "During recess, all the kids went out into the yard. Even though I was a bit shy, I forced myself to go outside to try and make a friend. But that wasn't easy, so I sat down all by myself, feigning indifference. Then some kid came over to me. The conversation began innocently enough, but soon he asked me why I'd beaten up his brother. I protested that I didn't know who his brother was, told him what he just said wasn't true.

"'Hey, Grami, this dude's calling me a liar,' the kid yelled out, and this huge lout, who looked like a chunk ripped from the side of one of the surrounding mountains, took a menacing step in my direction. I got the fright of my life. But at the same time, I realized there was only one escape from the situation. When the huge lout came up to me, I knew I had only one chance to strike. I slugged him in the mouth without warning, so hard he dropped to the ground like a sack of potatoes. His friend turned as white as a sheet. He quickly picked him up, and they both fled like headless chickens. From that day on, no one ever picked on me at that school again."

As I lay sprawled on the ground, my dad's story flashed through my mind. I didn't want to do it, but I knew I had to. I leaped from the ground as if jolted by lightning and kicked him hard in the shins. He was stunned. Then the tough boy everyone was afraid of all of a sudden began apologizing profusely to me. No one could believe it. From then on, even the other team members began to tread carefully around us, and every time they ran into me they apologized. That day, I became a hero among the group.

But not for long, because the group had more important heroes. Located at the end of our street was a local community hall that had pinball machines and a cinema. Every Saturday they showed films starring Bruce Lee, Stallone, Schwarzenegger, Chuck Norris, Jackie Chan, and other childhood idols. One Saturday they were going to show *Rocky IV*. Excitement and a sense of anticipation as to Rocky's latest adventures steadily mounted.

At the time, the Cold War was coming to an end, and in the film the Russians were portrayed as fanatics hungry for American blood. But at the end of the film, they were presented as humane in their recognition of democratic values and human rights. We didn't care about politics, however. All we cared about was Rocky's victory. He always took his fair share of punches, but was able to come back after almost being beaten to death and deliver his crushing blows. The archetypal movie character who rises up at the end of the film and heroically fights on behalf of the downtrodden exceeded all our expectations.

Survivor's "Eye of the Tiger" began to play. Rocky got back up and landed one blow after another . . . the hulking, invincible bully began to totter. A wave of excitement swept through the hall and I began pounding the chair in front of me with my fists. My hands were hurting, but I didn't stop because I wanted Rocky to win. I wanted the big bad Russian to go down, to be defeated for the sake of the poor, the hungry, the dispossessed. In mid-trance, I raised my head and glanced around in the semidarkness of the cinema-hall. Everyone was doing the same thing. Everyone was pounding the seat in front of them. We were united, we were as one, carried along by a common desire, a common idea, a common dream.

And then America won.

▶▶ 1986 ◀◀

"The Final Countdown"—Europe

I SAW THEM on TV, and from that day on, the song went round and round in my head. I decided to buy their cassette, but kids back then didn't have pocket money. I'd heard of the term "allowance," but believe me, in socialist countries something like that was just a myth, as it was unthinkable for a kid to possess money. At best, we were given a bit of loose change to buy some chewing gum or a soft drink. Asking my dad for money seemed out of the question. So I decided to skimp on the chewing gum for a few weeks and try to save up the money that way.

I stood at the counter of the cassette shop with the money in my hand. When they handed me the cassette, I felt as if they were giving me the Holy Grail. The cover depicted the band members leaving planet Earth, and to me it seemed as if they were flying directly into my mind. The cassette player boomed out with unprecedented force, within me it fueled dreams of something bigger, something grander. I replayed the first song over and over again and . . . that afternoon, sitting in my dad's room, which was his own private world, so remote and inaccessible was it, I saw it as the conquest of new territories of the mind, as my own personal "Final Countdown," a dream of togetherness, unity, and mutual understanding, something that eluded not only the two of us, but the whole country as well.

But the world kept turning, the clock was counting down: 10, 9, 8 . . . we were getting ready.

"What do you need this for?" my mom asked when she found the switchblade in my backpack.

"For self-defense. Everyone in our group's got one," I replied, in puzzlement, as if she had asked me why I needed a soccer ball or a bicycle.

"It's dangerous," she said, and to this day, I'm still not sure how she managed to hide that switchblade without me noticing, stashing it someplace; I never found out where.

. . . 7, 6, 5, 4 . . . we got in the car. My sister and I sat on the backseat, which was covered with the obligatory bed sheet, as was customary on the long journey to the seaside.

. . . 3, 2, 1 . . . we were off to the seaside! My mom couldn't keep her eyes off me. I felt embarrassed, but I knew how much it meant to her: the first summer we had spent together since I was three, the first vacation my dad had agreed we could go on together.

It hadn't been so long ago that I first "met" her, maybe a year before that vacation. Before that, she had been "the woman who sent me parcels." I always looked forward to getting those gifts, and felt a little guilty about never writing to thank her. All those wonderful crayons and pens, delicious cakes, toys, and letters that to me were a mixture of both joy and sorrow, but to which I couldn't put any face. And so that's why I put to them the face of my aunt or my best friend Hare's mom. Whenever I went over to Hare's place, I'd make believe that his parents were mine, that I was part of a whole, rather than divided in two . . . My mom was also split in two—now that I'm a parent, I know that. But what we didn't know was that the country was also split between those who believed in it and those who wanted to break away from it. To those in the former group, the idea of breaking away was akin to condemning yourself to being an orphan, and that was unthinkable to them.

We in Bosnia were part of that half of the people who believed in Yugoslavia. In no other republic did people swear by the name of our "Dear Tito!" and in no other republic had the spirit of togetherness developed in the way it did in Bosnia.

"Let me take over now," I said to my friend Maher. I was turning the lamb on a spit in his yard for the end of Ramadan feast. We took turns, and whenever an older member of his family came outside, he would give us a few coins. We'd be beside ourselves with joy, and we'd turn the spit even harder and faster. After a job well done, we were rewarded with a bit of flatbread and a piece of lamb that we ate with relish. We had full stomachs and full hearts. We were happy and content, just like at Easter when we cracked red eggs with each other. We shared and celebrated everything together, both Christmas and Ramadan, always with each another, until they separated us.

Every evening that summer, in the year of "Our Lord and Savior Tito" 1986, we sat in the yard of the house belonging to my mom's aunt on the island of Hvar, playing cards.

Just thirty feet down below us, the choppy sea gnawed away at the rocks, providing an abundant breeding ground for the mosquitoes. The noise of the crickets was outdone only by Metallica's "Orion" on our little cassette player, beginning softly and mysteriously, and then blasting through air thick with the smell of bug spray.

"You plays good," my best friends from Hvar—two Hungarian brothers from Vojvodina—said in broken Serbian to my cousin, a drummer from Belgrade, as we listened to demo tapes by his band, Revolt.

Summer ended. We loaded up all our things into our Zastava 101. As we drove off, we turned our heads to take one last look at the house. Someone had scrawled graffiti on the wall, which read, "Faggot House." Quite simply we were the wrong people in the wrong place.

►► 1987 ◄◄

"Where the Streets Have No Name"—U2

THAT WINTER THE TEMPERATURE dropped below -20°C, but it didn't prevent my dad from taking me skiing on Mount Jahorina.

The song "Where the Streets Have No Name," which was playing on the old cassette player of our green 1982 Lada Riva, sounded as if it was coming from afar. The rhythmic sound of the guitar mixed with the hum of the car going up the mountain road as the snow-covered evergreen trees sped past. My dad deliberately jerked the steering wheel left and right, causing the car to skid and spin toward the shoulders of the road covered with huge deposits of snow, while we nearly split our sides laughing. I was happy.

The next song that came on was "Don't You (Forget about Me)" by Simple Minds, but forgetting was something inevitable and life went on. Fast-forward to 2001 and once again, for the first time in ten years, I was in my old homeland. My aunt was waiting for me at the bus station. She was still quite plump and she still couldn't stop talking, apart from when she took a deep drag on one of the Filter 57 cigarettes that always dangled from the corner of her mouth. The green packaging and the small red dragon on the cigarette pack—as a kid I used to think the dragon was a little frog—irresistibly reminded me of a swamp surrounded by the cloud of smoke in which my aunt was always enveloped.

Had I known that that would be the last time I ever saw her, maybe I would have told her how much she meant to me. Even when she sewed brightly colored patches over the holes in my deliberately torn jeans. I never wore them again after that. Yes, maybe I would have told her that I loved her even when she urged me to hang out with the "nerds," whom I found unbelievably boring and avoided like the plague.

In 1987, the kids on my street were mostly hard cases rather than nerds. "Want to make some trouble?" asked one of those hard cases who today no longer exist, having been killed by a Serb mortar shell fired out of sheer Balkan spite on the first day of Sarajevo's liberation. Fittingly, we called him Beljo (Trouble). He was the embodiment of a street life that was hard, but fair, governed by unwritten laws and rules that every kid obeyed.

"Now," Hare cried, and with all our might we tossed lumps of dirt mixed with berries that splattered the white-haired man's balcony with red dye. It was our revenge on him for breaking our sled because he said we made too much racket out the front of his apartment. Nobody wrote the natural laws of street life, but all the kids respected them in order to maintain the peaceful equilibrium among the residents.

In 2001 my streets had no name. They had different names that to me were unfamiliar. The people around me were unfamiliar too, apart from my girlfriend, who firmly gripped my hand. "Why are your hands so cold?" she asked, but she already knew the answer to that. From the moment she embarked on this uncertain journey with me, she knew that my heart was clenched so tight that it no longer pumped heat into my body.

"I dreamed of those streets every night for years, but they were realer in my dreams than in reality," I later told her, after we left a city no longer mine and my streets that had no name were far behind us. Maybe it's better to leave them back there.

Before that, we genuinely believed that we were moving forward. But we also knew how to laugh at our own expense. In the '80s, we compared the one-time success of our "Brotherhood and

3 MINUTES AND 53 SECONDS

Unity" project with the then reality. A perfect expression of that comparison was *A Better Life*, the Yugoslav TV series.[1]

My grandad didn't want to watch it because he felt it insulted the Yugoslavia for which he had taken bullets, lost relatives, and languished in prison on Goli Otok island. And maybe it was out of similar pique that he preferred to watch *Dynasty*, the American TV series which, no matter how remote it was from the lives of ordinary Yugoslavs, still offered some sort of appeal, probably suggestive of what in the coming decades was to become our dream too: the Pan-American dream.

But other than the dizzying effect of the opening credits of *Dynasty*, we kids got nothing out of those TV series. We were interested in wild, untamed, endless play. We were boisterous, full of energy, and we needed an outlet.

When Guns 'n' Roses entered our lives something resonated within us. The times were about to erupt. People didn't know what the future held, but they still believed in the preservation of the old ways. My cousin was part of the in-between generation.

"Turn that racket off!" he yelled, bursting into his room once, when I was visiting him, and turned off the tape at the best part of "Welcome to the Jungle," just as the snarling menace of the song enters your world and fills the whole of space with soaring guitars, smoke and fire, guns and roses . . .

"Listen to something better," he told me, putting on another cassette. And as the room filled with the sound of Idoli, a New Wave band from Belgrade, which I found totally boring and too commercial, I went into another room, and there I continued to dream of my idols. I took out a pen from the rucksack that I brought with me on weekends whenever I stayed over at my aunt's place, and started to draw the band's skull and crossbones logo on my skin.

My appetite for destruction was overwhelming.

---

[1] *Bolji život*, a mix of soap opera, comedy, and drama, revolving around the Popadić family and their struggle to adapt to the rapid political and economic changes taking place in post-Tito Yugoslavia —*Translator's note*.

▶▶ 1988 ◀◀

"Seventh Son of a Seventh Son"—Iron Maiden

NINETEEN EIGHTY-EIGHT was a year of heavy metal. I'm not talking about the quality of the local drinking water, which probably no one in Yugoslavia monitored at that time. We trusted everything we consumed and everything we absorbed via our five senses. There was no doubt it was good—as long as it was ours. But, okay, I admit there were those who didn't believe in Yugoslavia quite so blindly. And with good reason too—the times were heavy, and getting heavier, just like the music.

At the time when heavy metal entered my life, wearing patches was popular. I didn't know half the bands, but their logos—skeletons, skulls, guns, guitars—seemed to me sufficient reason for them to emblazon my denim jacket. I did know Iron Maiden, however, and I liked them. Their epic themes, rousing rhythms, and soaring vocals speak perfectly to young souls that are insecure and still seeking their place in the world. Those patches often landed me in trouble.

"Hand over your money!" Hare and I were ambushed by the gang known as "Korea," who operated in the area around the Eternal flame—the World War II memorial—and the Sarajka Shopping Center. I gave the impression of being a tough guy, which actually I wasn't, and that's probably what provoked them. But maybe they attacked me because they didn't take kindly to the idea of me wearing satanic heavy metal logos while standing near the war memorial. It insulted their almost Oriental sense of propriety. Unfortunately, they didn't reveal whether they were of a pro-communist or a pro-American political persuasion, as they were too busy kicking my teeth in. Joking aside, they beat me up for my money, and when that's up for grabs, all sense of propriety becomes secondary.

There were many times when I wanted to believe I was a street kid, because in one sense I think I genuinely was. After my grandma died, my grandad withdrew into himself and I lost my most loyal companion. He spent most of his time at the War Veterans' Club, a sacred place for those who'd served in World War II, where they played bocce and cards. My grandad would almost invariably lose those games. Much later, I found out that they could see his cards reflected in the photochromic lenses of his glasses, the type that darkened automatically beneath the bare bulbs in the club's smoke-filled rooms.

Who knows, maybe that was just something my dad made up out of envy, because everyone knew my grandad to be a "human calculator"—he could multiply large numbers quickly without batting an eye, and he could spot a mistake in rows of digits without the aid of a computer. But above all, like a magician, he always managed to find me four-leaf clovers. All he needed to do was look in a clover meadow and he'd find one!

However, after he ended up alone, he became merely a shadow of his former self. This new grandad got angry at me for no reason, threw ashtrays at me, but he also knew how to protect me from the wrath of my dad, who was disappointed at being twice divorced, and whose children had been scattered God only knows where.

My grandad smoked three packs a day, while for me it was like smoking one pack a month, given the passive smoke I inhaled. But every now and then, I would light one up too, if only to try to capture its alluring effect. One day I was sitting alone, a cigarette and a lighter in front of me, an empty glass beside me. I lit up and took a drag. The taste, which I couldn't define, but which I'd later compare to burning metal and rubber, made my mouth fill with saliva. I began to salivate like crazy. That's what the glass was for. I spat and puffed. It was disgusting, but I had to go through with it. It was a necessary part of growing up alone.

I grew up on the street, with all its rules. But I wasn't a lout. I never have been. My gentle exterior prevented me from becoming one. Besides, I was fiercely loyal to my friends and to the group. I'd never betray them, not for anything in the world. I would have given them everything I owned—sometimes I even did. Every leather soccer ball my dad brought back for me after attending medical seminars in Europe I unselfishly shared with the other members of our group, every tennis racket, every tennis ball—and I always ended up with nothing. All of them got lost in the bushes on the slopes of our street in hilly Sarajevo. And sometimes the shiny, colorful, leather soccer balls quickly ended up just becoming nothing but deflated checkers. But that's how all of us lived: not recognizing private ownership and dedicated to the common good. And if anyone violated that unwritten rule—well, all the worse for them.

The group fell silent and the dancing abruptly stopped. We were celebrating Vedo's birthday at his place, and everything was going great. The capitalist Coca-Cola went perfectly with the socialist pretzels that we dipped in our glasses, producing an exciting, frothy chemical reaction. We were listening to music, and then in stark contrast to the seriousness and epic grandeur of my favorite song—"Seventh Son"—Salt-N-Pepa's "Push It" came on the cassette player, a plain, simple, infectious, playful, sexual song . . . the song was everything that heavy metal wasn't, but I thought sounded totally wicked, and so I was ashamed of myself. But that wasn't the reason for the shock. The silence came after one of our friends looked under the bed to retrieve a pretzel, and dragged out a spanking new tennis racket, fresh tennis balls, uninflated soccer balls, and God knows what else! The spirit of sharing had been betrayed. I never looked at Vedo the same way again, and from that moment on, I was quite reserved toward him.

But the group as a whole didn't change. It always found ways to move forward, to forget, to restore its energy through games, through new rules and new ways of playing. Vedo decided to share some of his tennis balls with us. We welcomed his initiative by gathering a few potato sacks and tying them together into a tennis net. The game continued.

It seemed that the group as a whole always lived according to the spirit of another popular song of the time, "Don't Worry, Be Happy," while at the same time the world was slowly preparing for the collapse of the Soviet Union and the fall of socialism. Yugoslavia was trying to maintain its own self-governing social-ism, and failing miserably. "Be Worry, Don't Happy," as Rambo Amadeus would say many years later. Everything became more pressing.

The economic reforms of 1988, a last-ditch effort to revive the all but collapsing Yugoslav, economy, did not succeed. Even back then, signs were appearing that Yugoslavia's nationalist and socio-economic uncertainties would lead to a state of emergency, but we were completely unaware of it.

To us kids, Yugoslavia was indestructible and more powerful than ever before. As for the economy . . . we knew how to deal with that as well.

Yasser was celebrating his birthday with a circus theme and, in the spirit of the new socio-capitalist times, he invited us to take part by performing some sort of an act. As the most jovial and the most inventive member of the gang, Hare immediately accepted. He did a clown number in which he stumbled about, performed a pantomime, rode a bike hands-free while falling over again and again. We rolled around in hysterics.

"And now," Yasser announced theatrically, with a look of pure satisfaction on his face at the success of his self-organized circus (which is what Yugoslavia itself actually was at the time), "I invite you to take part in a competition!" We were all flabbergasted. The word "competition" echoed in our heads like a promise in the form of a sweet delicious lollipop, a shiny new toy, or the soccer and tennis balls we dreamed about. Instead, Yasser explained that we had to buy a ticket to win. We cried foul.

"On every ticket," Yasser continued without hesitation, "there's a number. And each number corresponds to a toy." Hope returned to us. Wary, but tempted by the chance of winning something nice, we gave him the money. The first few tickets had no winners, but we'd come to learn that all games of chance were like that—you win some, you lose some.

And in fact, Hare won a shoddy toy truck that badly needed a new coat of paint. Fatty was delighted by the half-used notebook with Smurfs on the cover. And I won a toy Red Indian with one of its arms broken off. Several of the others won similar prizes, but then again, it was better than nothing, which is what a lot of them ended up with. The group wasn't happy. Serious arguments erupted over who got what, and over whether Yasser had cheated us. He defended his entrepreneurial spirit, and told us that such was our luck.

Then his mom appeared, a strict but fair-minded woman of whom Yasser was deathly afraid, like fire. When she found out what he'd done, she gathered up all our old, shoddy toys, and brought out a box with newer and much nicer toys. She marked them with numbers and made tickets where there were no losers, bar one—her own son, who all the while sat with his arms folded and a scowl on his face, while the group thanked their lucky stars.

Yasser was ahead of his time. He was the embodiment of what many years later would become commonplace in all the former-Yugoslav republics—brute capitalism, a transition without end, in which all were left to fend for themselves and survive as best they could, lying, cheating, doing whatever it took.

The state no longer protected us, it didn't actively discourage those who wanted to do harm, didn't put a damper on their dirty dealings, didn't give the losers a second chance.

I fared better than my friends—I survived the breakup of my home and, with the death of Yugoslavia, I got a mom. But overnight people became orphans abandoned to the winds of time.

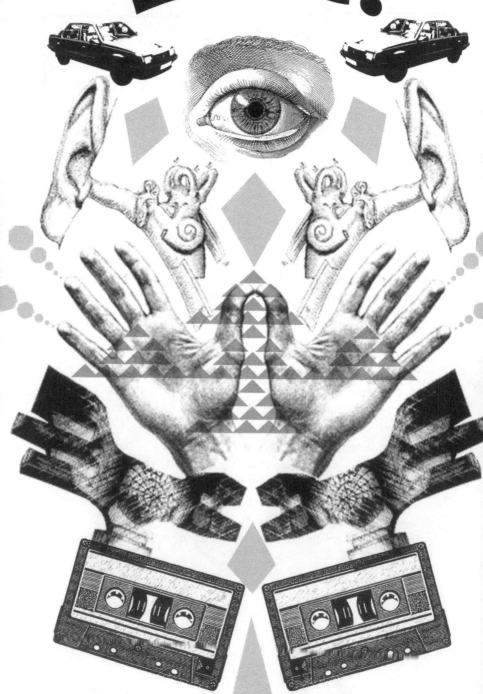

▶▶ 1989 ◀◀

"Epic"—Faith No More

YUGOSLAVIA FINALLY WON the Eurovision! But why? If you believe the conspiracy theories, there is a hidden meaning in the fact that Yugoslavia won the Eurovision—a politically and ideologically motivated event—just before its collapse, at a time when the country was in economic, social, political, inter-ethnic disarray . . .

Even so, the winning song, "Rock Me Baby," was not as popular as the following year's entry, "*Hajde da ludujemo*" (Let's Go Crazy) by Tajči. But it was enough to secure our victory and for national joy to erupt in the midst of difficult times.

I wasn't interested in the Eurovision, although I still watched it, like everyone else. But there was always something about it that turned me off, something to do with the gaudy colors and lights and the shallow song lyrics, which lodged in my mind like a mantra. In contrast, "Epic" by Faith No More appealed to me from the very first time I heard it.

Who can forget that scene in the music video with the all-seeing eye in the middle of the hand shooting out blood? What was that for? Nobody knew. But the eye was there, and it saw and knew more than us. Faith No More would eventually come to be known as pioneers of rap-metal. By temporarily uniting these two genres, it made me feel less self-conscious of the fact that sometimes I really liked rap.

The unforgettable riff ripped through my ears and I stared at the scenes of a dying fish and an exploding piano in wide-eyed amazement. At the same time, the words of the song rang inside my head while random music videos appeared on the screen with the famous MTV logo in the corner.

MTV was still a channel that played just music videos, and the most shocking program it showed was *Headbangers Ball*. Everything that was loud, controversial or outrageous to older people was shown on that show. But later, in the '90s, when eccentricity became mainstream, the show lost its edge, and the alternative scene became part of everyday life. But we weren't yet ready for that.

We started going to discos. I didn't know what to do at a disco except sit in a corner and watch. I didn't like the music they played. It was some sort of funk-rap. The vision of the future at that time was robots moving to a breakdance beat. Our group of friends became obsessed with dancing to pre-choreographed steps, and it all just looked fake to me.

I was sitting with my arms folded next to Jasmina—my first crush as far as I can remember—drinking Coke, when the thought struck me that I had to do something. I leaned back and stretched, and, as if by accident, put my hand on her arm. A surprise awaited me. My hand brushed against someone else's hand. I turned around and saw that my friend Skipper was trying to do the same thing as me. We locked eyes for a moment and quickly pulled our hands away. Jasmina ended up without a date, and the disco went wild to the robotic rap of Grandmaster Flash.

The realization that I had a crush on the same girl as my friend, whom I considered to be the leader of our group, the key decision maker, the one who was always in the right, really messed with my head. After that, I tried to steer clear of her, tried hard not to stare at her dark eyes, which was difficult because I was constantly out on the street—the first one out, the last one in.

There was something poetic about the fact that she was the last person from our group of friends I saw as I was getting into my dad's car with my skateboard.

"You'll have to go live with your mom for a while," my dad

said, after coming to blows with my grandad, who then stormed off to the War Veterans' Club. "Until I find us a new place to live. I'll pack your clothes, you pack a couple of your favorite things, I don't know, a toy or something . . ."

It was all so confusing. I loved my grandad, but I had to obey my dad. I took the first thing I laid my eyes on in my room—my skateboard. "I'll be back here soon enough, anyway," I thought to myself, not knowing that what I held in my hand was a one-way ticket. Because after my departure the war would begin, and my dad would flee to another country and start a new family before we ever saw each other again.

Jasmina was outside, playing tennis. She turned around and waved at me. After that her face, along with the image of my city, disappeared forever in the rear window of the car. Fade out. The end.

The '90s were in sight, a new decade was upon us. However, it held no hope for a better future. Black clouds were gathering over our heads, the prelude to a rain of lead, storms of explosions, and children's screams deep in the night. I was saved from the storm, but some of my friends weren't so lucky.

That decade was the most exciting of my life, but at the same time the loneliest. The feeling of guilt at having left behind my friends would not let go of me. All the music in the world couldn't change that.

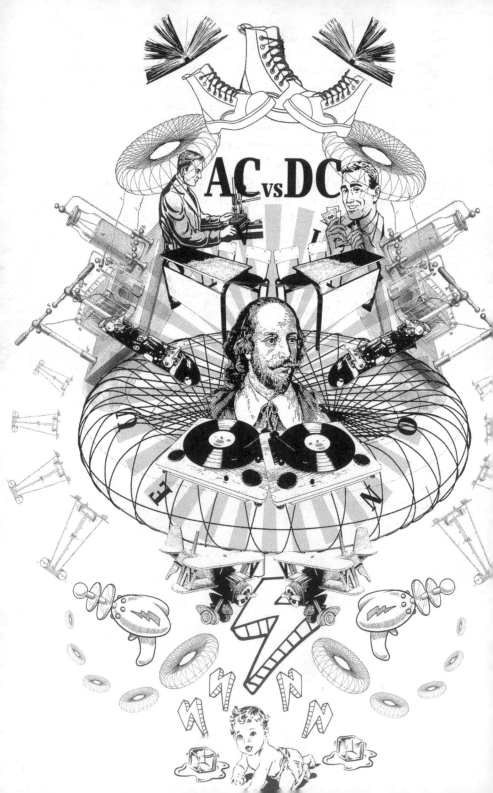

▶▶ 1990 ◀◀

"Ice Ice Baby"—Vanilla Ice

Toto cutugno won the Eurovision Song Contest with the song *Insieme*, but we were farther away than ever from being "together."

I was living in Skopje. Summer break had ended and I was preparing to return to Sarajevo. Although it was strange that my dad hadn't called me all summer, not even for my birthday, I decided not to think about it. I had work to do—I had to pack my clothes and, yes, my skateboard too. I couldn't forget that. I didn't have many other things.

I sat there in readiness to hit the road, and waited for my mom to get home from work. She was stunned when she saw me. She didn't understand what was going on. I told her that I would be going to Sarajevo for a while to see my friends, but that I would return at the first opportunity.

"Where will you stay?" she asked, as if in shock.

"Well, at home," I replied, in confusion.

"But, you live here now . . ."

Most of the words we hear in life are meaningless and forgettable, but some words change your life forever. "I live here now" became my mantra in the coming years and I did everything I could for it to be truly the case.

I gave up my language, my customs, and the person I used to be. My natural sociability turned into a desire for solitude. My dislike of books turned into a love of books. My lackadaisical study habits turned into obsessive studiousness. I turned from being one person into another. I don't know whether or not that was a good thing, but what I do know is that it was necessary.

After several months spent in self-imposed "isolation," I began to go out again. There was a Goth club in Debar Maalo called "Doors," a mystical, magical place. Candles burned inside and it smelled of incense. There for the first time I got to know the Macedonian alternative music scene, which wasn't well known in the rest of Yugoslavia. Apart from the famous rock group *Leb i Sol*, we hadn't heard of anyone else. In general, Macedonia was fairly marginal within Yugoslavia, and as the years passed that began to piss me off.

My life turned into a struggle for the rights of the disadvantaged, the victims, the silent and unobtrusive, the condemned, the abandoned, the forgotten, the neglected. I wanted Macedonia to be recognized and respected, but that wasn't often the case. Me and my new homeland were pretty much snubbed by everyone, and all we could do was work on ourselves—obsessively, and with great sacrifice and devotion. And if others recognized us for it, then good for them.

One night, my sister and her boyfriend, Bobby, decided to take me to the movies in order to drag me out of my self-imposed isolation and away from my negative thoughts. The film was called *Green Card*. It was playing at the small theatre on the first floor of the Macedonian Cultural Center. The lights dimmed and the movie started. Comfortably seated, with popcorn and drinks in hand, we were suddenly startled by the sound of loud drumming. On the screen, a boy in the subway was pounding away on a plastic bucket with incredible drumming skill. The film continued and, even though it was supposed to be a romantic comedy, it exposed many social truths about America. Maybe it just wanted to erase white people's guilt of racial and social tension in America. Nevertheless, it was a great example of filmmaking from the '90s, a time when the entertainment industry still cared about its audience and not just their money.

In seventh grade, they put me in what was called the

"Serbian class" because my knowledge of Macedonian wasn't good enough. I came from Sarajevo, a city that fostered a spirit of unity. I didn't even know which of my friends was a Serb, a Croat, a Muslim, an Austro-Hungarian. So I found it especially strange that a class made up of people of all sorts of nationalities—just like a mini-Yugoslavia—were lumped together under the label of just one of those nations. There were nine of us in total. And it was hell!

At my new school in Skopje, I felt a sense of fear and dread in every class. You could be given a test at any moment, on any day of the week. And to my amazement everyone knew the answers to everything. In the first SC, CS or Serbo-Croatian class (and every other variant of the title), the teacher introduced herself and immediately proceeded to test my knowledge.

The teacher was an elderly woman with pink lipstick smudged above and below her lips. She was an old-school Soviet-style teacher, although without a rod in her hand. She interrogated me thoroughly, while I remained close-mouthed and silent. Exasperated, the desperate woman began to sweat and to squawk, with steam coming out of her ears and nose.

My throat clenched and I looked down at my seat. I covered my face with my hair, which even back then was long, as tears dripped from my eyes. Drip, drip, slowly and quietly . . .

People say "still waters run deep." Those tears etched grooves in my brain, which then all of a sudden snapped into life. I became infuriated, I wanted to break, smash, destroy, burn—not the teacher or the school, but myself.

The fact that my dad had made his own life easier by getting my teachers to give me A's so that he wouldn't have to concern himself about my education was rather shameless on his part. But what about my own sense of shame? From that moment on, I decided that things had to change. And so in seventh grade I began to study: "A, B, C, D . . ."

Around the clock, without going out, without sleeping, without playing—I studied until my head hurt. And suddenly I realized that I could do it, that I knew how to, that I was worth it . . . and that's the most important realization a young mind can ever reach. You don't need others to believe in you, as long as you have faith in yourself.

At school I had a friend who looked a little like Vanilla Ice—tall and blond, with a pompadour hairstyle. Physically we were total opposites, but we soon became best friends. We sat together in class and were rarely apart, even outside school—either he was at my place or I was at his. Sometimes he got teased because he was tall and awkward, and that would make me blind with rage. His name was Timur and he was my best friend. And more than that, most probably he was a substitute for all the friends from Sarajevo I had lost and whom I would never see again.

At the time, "Ice Ice Baby" was the hit song that was driving people crazy, some with joy, others with despair. I remember that several of us from my neighborhood were at my place, and when "Ice Ice Baby" started playing, we just went wild. Timur was doing his famous arm-flapping dance. That is, he would open and close his denim jacket with his hands while throwing his head back and forth like a bird.

Timur was a boy who dreamed of building lasers, airplanes, spaceships, and who wrote science-fiction stories. He used to buy *Galaxy*, a magazine dedicated to science and technology. I started collecting new and old editions of the magazine too. I can honestly say that I learned all the basics of science from those magazines, because their content was expert and objective. Even today, when there's excitement or furor over some natural phenomenon or other, and everyone goes half-crazy with fear, an old logical and scientific article from *Galaxy* comes to mind, and I just smile to myself.

We talked about astronomy and the universe. We knew which of the planets had rings and moons, how many they were, what their maximum and minimum temperatures were, whether or not it rained sulfuric acid or whether there was evidence for the existence of water on them. We knew everything about the universe. However, we knew nothing about girls.

But who needs girls when you've dedicated yourself to science , , , and when there's some good music playing in the background, of course. But music was also changing. MTV Unplugged was born, and I bought my first record: *The Razors Edge* by AC/DC. The song "Thunderstruck" and the sound of the records themselves hit me like a real thunderbolt. I was addicted.

I didn't have the money to buy records, but I desperately wanted them. My mom gave me money to buy my lunch at 7, a fast-food joint, because she thought it would make it easier for me to fit in. But I kept the money instead. Going hungry each day was a small price to pay to buy a new record each week.

"Where did you get so many new records from?" Mom finally asked, and that put an end to me "buying" my lunch. That's how the legend of my lunchbox pies began, for which I became famous at school.

Some of us lived for music and progressive ideas. Smiki was one of them. He was the future founder of the band SAF. He wore Doc Martens and listened to noise metal in seventh grade. A rumor circulated about him that once, when he was in hospital with a broken bone, out of boredom he read the Bible from cover to cover in just two days. And on occasion, he would recite lines from a Shakespeare play in the original English.

But Smiki was one in a million. And our country was interested not in progressive children, but in really retrograde ideas. People began talking openly about ethnic conflict. To us kids, the idea of a nation being torn apart was unthinkable (because to us Yugoslavia was a single nation). We were a single united entity. But older people, who recalled a different Yugoslav past, knew differently. And they were to be proven right.

We rode the wave of carefree youth while we could. But not for long.

►►1991◄◄

"Losing My Religion"—R.E.M.

TEEN SPIRIT RULED our lives and I lived for the weekends, when we had jam sessions with our friends from junior high. Kečer introduced me to hardcore punk and bands with weird names that were borderline funny and had that necessary dose of rejecting society's norms, which perfectly matched my own rebellious spirit.

A chewed-up cassette was spitting out a refrain from "My God Rides a Skateboard" by German band Spermbirds. This was followed by the screaming vocals of "Americans are Cool—Fuck You!" a song that protested the spread of American-style democracy all over the world. The Americans themselves didn't give a damn about any of it.

It was the middle of the Gulf War. The adults watched events unfold on TV as if they were part of an evening thriller, completely removed from the lives of the Iraqi people, who, by the way, weren't dying at the hands of the dictator from whom the Americans wished to liberate them, but were being killed by American bombs. In reality, however, something quite different was taking place, both globally and locally. Unrest began to stir in Yugoslavia. All of a sudden, the present turned from being precarious to completely uncertain, and no one so much as contemplated the future.

"Why shouldn't I wear this T-shirt?" I protested.

"Because it's wrong," my mom said.

"Says who?"

"Not to mention it's dangerous."

Our argument went on. In the end, I decided not to wear the Bad Religion T-shirt with a crossed-out cross printed on it. I'd borrowed it from Kečer for Easter "celebrations" at the main Cathedral. I decided against wearing it, not out of fear, but so that my mom would stop worrying. But what did I know about religion? To me it was a sign of conformism and an inability to think for yourself. Besides which, religion could in no way be reconciled with science, the thing I really venerated.

"Big Bang" by Bad Religion was playing in the background. I was thinking about the origin of the world, the universe, and our place within it. Everything seemed perfectly fine to me, but at the same time completely meaningless. Science, with its laws and principles, provided some comfort, bringing order to the chaos in which we found ourselves.

Religion found a place in my life, but only years later, when I realized that atheism is just another form of fanaticism. At the same time, I wasn't interested in "isms," either religious or political. Unlike myself, our country was overrun by chauvinism. One wrong word, one nasty look, or even just having the wrong surname was enough to get you beaten up.

Snuff's "I Think We're Alone Now"—a cover of the Tiffany song from the happier and less serious '80s—was a track often played on *Maximum Rocknroll*, an alternative music program on Macedonian Radio 2. Standing by in readiness, I pressed "record" on the cassette player. Soon our small country would be alone now too, but also sovereign and independent. And then our struggles would be ours alone.

I played a few chords on the guitar and Fatty seemed to like them. Kečer tapped the cymbal suspended from the light fitting because, as in true DIY punk rock style, there was no stand. Then he tapped the single snare drum and the familiar hard-core "bupp-u-dupp-u-dupp" beat filled my bedroom. Fatty was recording us on an old cassette player. He plucked his acoustic guitar as if it were a bass, while we kept playing madly. We had no focus, no guiding message or vision, and our songs were made up on the spot. And in the spirit of parody and social consciousness that characterized the punk movement, we were called Social Imbecility. Like true punks, we had no idea how to play, but we loved it—more than anything else.

As a kid, I'd hated guitar lessons at the Sarajevo Music Academy. But later, as a teenager, I was glad that I'd learned to play an instrument. Soon, though, all I had left was my classical guitar. I had to return the electric guitar I'd borrowed—just when Kečer bought himself a great big drum kit, and just when a bass player joined our rehearsals. Those two kept on playing, and later formed the band Superhicks. They're probably the only band in Macedonia today that dares to engage in any intelligent social criticism, while, ironically, those who are the actual object of their critique bop along to their songs.

The thing that Kečer didn't like was my soft spot for heavy metal. But what could I do when Metallica released their last good album that year, and the sound was heavy—heavy and slow—too slow for hardcore punks. In the end, the only thing that I have left from my punk period is a demo cassette tape of our songs with a homemade cover and the "SK-HC" (Skopje Hardcore) graffiti tag on my garage wall.

However, many years later, when I began to write seriously, that ideal of the perfect hardcore punk song came back to life in my writing—something fast, furious, short, as short as possible, which says everything and leaves nothing unsaid. I'm still chasing that ideal.

We were in the front row at a concert being held outside the former Central Committee of the League of Communists of Macedonia, now the government building. Bobby lifted me onto his shoulders and I was right there—a few meters away from Goran Tanevski from the band Mizar. The sounds of "Svjat Dreams" floated over the sea of people around me and we were united by his heavy, serious voice and the heavy drums that echoed in our ears and reverberated through our bodies, proud of "Macedonia, our motherland."

▶▶ 1992 ◀◀

"Killing in the Name"—RATM

ANOTHER WORLD OF SOUND was slowly but surely entering my life. While hardcore punk forever remained on the sidelines, garage rock broke out of the underground and directly entered the minds of millions of young people around the world, changing the music scene forever. Taking our cue from Nirvana, we wore plaid shirts or T-shirts over long-sleeved shirts, while Pearl Jam, with their more melodic sound, epitomized the American reality of the '90s.

"Did you know that you look like the lead singer from the Red Hot Chili Peppers?" my classmates teased me. I was crazy about their album *Blood Sugar Sex Magik*. Alternative funk rock with shades of rap was a revelation to me.

The eclectic '90s had begun. "Give It Away" was rocking from my cassette player. I copied out the lyrics, even though I didn't really understand them, nor did I read too deeply into the words that preached altruism and selflessness. To me they signified rebellion and a "don't-give-a-damn" attitude. The times were mean and nasty. The war and the siege of my birthplace had begun.

May 9, 1992. Victory Day, commemorating the end of World War II and the defeat of fascism. We had to write about the same topic for an assignment in school and I couldn't restrain myself. Risking a good grade, I wrote about fascism and my sense of loss, about the death of Yugoslavia built on the skeletons of those who'd fought against fascism, which in former Yugoslavia had become even more pronounced than it had been in 1942. I wrote about my friends and my fear of never seeing them again. I got an A for my assignment, even though I digressed from the topic slightly, but what else could I do when the times were going awry?

Timur was attacked. He'd been getting harassed for some time by the nouveau-riche kids—real turncoat nationalist bastards—who burned the teachers' grade books and scrawled graffiti over the school and yet somehow still got top grades. The day's classes were over, and just outside the schoolyard, a mob had gathered. They followed Timur, teasing him. He bore it stoically, but then they began shoving and hitting him. He tried to defend himself but he lost his balance. He fell to the ground and the others jumped on him. At that moment, I forgot that they were all two heads taller than me and twice as heavy as my eighty-odd pounds—including the weight of my denim jacket covered with heavy metal patches—and I threw myself into the fray, swinging wildly at everyone around me.

Timur got up and, not realizing that I was there, he ran away. A few of the others gave chase but he was a lot faster and they couldn't catch him. Someone shouted "You fucking Serb!" which couldn't have been farther from the truth. Some of them came back and turned on me. "This guy was sticking up for him!" they shouted, and in that instant, time stood still. Moving toward me was a force of nature in the shape of a crowd hungry for blood.

"Don't lay a finger on him!" came a voice from nearby. They froze to the spot and then turned tail and left. I looked behind me and saw a hard, mean-looking metalhead. He gave me a wink. To this day I don't know who he was—maybe my heavy metal guardian angel—but I'm grateful to him because he saved me from a lynching. I'd always known it, but that day I received indisputable confirmation: music binds us together regardless of ethnic, religious or regional differences.

Timur never forgave himself for abandoning me, even though at the time and amid the confusion, he hadn't realized it was me in there, trying to defend him. Since then he's been trying to make up for it and he's always been there when I needed him, to this very day. But then, I reckon it's because I helped him when everyone else abandoned him, and because we were different from all the others—prejudged and misunderstood. Maybe that's why we were inseparable in good times and in bad. And the bad times were yet to come.

The next day Bobby and his brother came to school with me and hung around the schoolyard in case they needed to defend us. Both of them were big and burly, unshaven, long-haired guys. The Principal called us to her office.

"Who are those thugs hanging around the schoolyard?" she yelled at us. We were taken aback.

"M-my sister's boyfriend," I stammered.

"Tell them to leave at once!" she thundered.

"But yesterday Timur got beaten up, and we—"

"I'm not interested. I don't know anything about that. And you two will be punished . . ."

Of course she knew. Of course she was interested. But not in justice. She was interested in the parents of the kids who beat us up, in their support, their money, their power. We were worthless insects who, squashed or otherwise, made no difference to anyone. We were punished, while the bullies got off scot-free. That was the beginning of a new era.

I was checking out the cassettes at Bagi Shop, the music store in the Mavrovka mall, when all of a sudden, a thunderous sound from the speakers shook me to the core. I was electrified. I asked the owner what he was playing and before I knew what was happening, Rage Against the Machine entered my life like a tornado, lifting me up high and slamming me back down again. I felt as though I were riding a wild horse that I couldn't control. The times made all of us feel that way.

It was the end of the school year and we were getting ready for the holidays. The physics teacher hadn't arrived yet. The bell rang. Timur and I were arm wrestling. Even though I was winning thirteen to three, I still wanted to keep going. "If you bend your body, you'll use the deltoid muscle." We'd talked about our arm-wrestling techniques many times before, and we knew the Latin names of all the large muscles, because we lifted weights every day after school. Timur pumped up quickly and he didn't plan on stopping. In the years to come, he became a dangerous guy who defied the bullies, the drawn pistols, and the security gorillas outside the nightclubs. In the end, those who used to beat him up would run a mile as soon as they saw him.

As we were arm wrestling, I twisted my arm awkwardly, so when Timur pressed down his fist with all his might, my arm had nowhere to go and a bone snapped—just like in the movies. I lost consciousness but then came to, and saw my arm dangling. I grabbed hold of it and ran outside. Thus began the saga of my humeral fracture.

Waiting several hours with a broken arm at the City hospital, and then being saddled with a poorly fitted plaster cast. Removal of the crappy cast with a pair of old-fashioned pliers, because the hospital's drill wasn't working. Broken bones that hadn't healed properly. Vain attempts at separating them. An operation and a metal rod inserted in my arm.

Then, a damaged nerve, slow recovery, and atrophied muscles after removal of the cast. The whole summer holidays spent at a rehabilitation center in Kozle. Every day. Massaging muscles. Hot paraffin wax therapy for a stiff elbow. Nerve stimulation, physical therapy exercises. Infrared heat lamp. All in vain. Macedonia's top neurosurgeons advised me to travel to Slovenia for an operation.

"Listen, son, if you want to get better, you'll have to work at it," said a middle-aged man who attended the physiotherapy sessions with me.

"But the nerve isn't responding. It's dead."

"Take a look at my arm," he said, and raised it. "Can you see that? It moves."

"But—"

"Listen to what I'm telling you. I know all about it. I had the same thing as you: radialis nerve injury," he smiled. "Just keep exercising and don't stop. Either you can depend on a machine hoist to lift your arm or you can lift it yourself."

"But I can't lift it, not even half an inch!"

"Lift it with your brain! Lift it in your mind. And put a splint on your arm before going to bed at night and sleep with it on."

Rage Against the Machine's "Killing in the Name" was roaring through the speakers. The walls were shaking. They're being killed in the name of who? Suffering, death, misery, hunger, and disease . . . Are my friends OK? . . . Are they alive? . . . What about my dad? Do I really care about him? . . . Has he been able to escape? I wondered to myself. But the only sound that emerged, from deep within me, was a wild and primordial cry: "Aaaaaah!" as I tried with all my strength and mental power to lift my arm.

The sweat was running down my forehead but I just kept repeating, "The power of the mind! The power of the mind!" I needed all the pent-up anger and frustration, the noise and rage of all those fighting against the machine—grunge rockers, gangsta rappers, and metalheads—so I could defeat the metal rod in my arm. Fourteen stainless steel screws that went through my bone and pinched the nerves that had previously been removed from the muscle tissue and held in the assistant's rubber-gloved hands during surgery to bind the bones. And then finally it happened—my arm moved—a fraction of an inch.

The distance between zero and a fraction of an inch is greater than the distance between one inch and a yard. Then everything sped up. And preparations for the high-school entrance exams went smoothly. But the intricate movements of the fingers that allow one to hold a pen and write were still far beyond my abilities. "Everything's in the mind," I remembered. I learned to write with my left hand, and that's how I got into the Josip Broz Tito Senior High School.

If comrade Tito had been able to know what was happening to the land that he'd built, he would have been thankful that he wasn't alive. Or maybe not?

▶▶ 1993 ◀◀

"Insane in the Brain"—Cypress Hill

"LET'S GO TO the Bagdad Café," said Kečer.

"I don't feel like going there," I replied.

"C'mon, we'll head over to Džadžo later," he added. That sounded OK to me. We took off.

I didn't like the Bagdad Café, until it was superseded by the New Age Teahouse, which later became my favorite hangout. But Džadžo and 21 at the Trades Center were the perfect venues for me: grungy, authentic, alternative, minus the tea and intellectualism, and minus the philosophers and mystics, everything that was abhorrent to my heavy metal and punk rock mindset at the time. But a person changes over time and may even mature, as long as he's not chewed up and spat out by the daily grind and turned into something that no longer resembles himself, but rather everyone else—in one huge pot of red-pepper *ajvar* sauce.

The former Yugoslavia was mired in upheaval, in contrast to the Czech Republic and Slovakia, which had managed to separate peacefully. The world cared not a whit about the war in Yugoslavia, because to them we were not part of Europe but an outpost. We were "Balkanites," dirt on their shoes to be wiped from their consciousness. But why would they care when there were at least a dozen other civil wars going on in the world, about which they didn't care either. Guatemala, Angola,

Afghanistan, Sudan, Sri Lanka, Libya, Rwanda, Sierra Leone, Algeria, Tajikistan, Burundi . . . to name but a few.

Bad Religion's *Recipe for Hate* sounded like the perfect album title for that time, but I didn't like it. It felt to me as though hardcore punk was dead. But it had been resurrected in a different way in the songs of the post-punk bands like Fugazi or in the grunge sound of Mudhoney, whose music I listened to until it almost drove my family and my neighbors crazy.

Whitney Houston was screaming "I Will Always Love You" on the TV and I turned it off in disgust. I liked a different kind of screaming: loud punk screaming and the rattling of the cassette tapes, which was sometimes even louder than the music itself. Nirvana's follow-up album to *Nevermind* wasn't like that and their performance on *MTV Unplugged* disappointed me. It seemed as though grunge rock was in crisis. Alternative music did not come to an end with the decline in Nirvana's popularity, however. Primus's *My Name is Mud* brought a new sound and a new awareness to my life. So did Disciplina Kičme and other unusual bands, which I discovered on my weekly pilgrimage, walking all the way from Debar Maalo to the Pop Top cassette shop on the concourse of the new railway station.

Despite the objections of my music buddy, Vlad, music could be both heavy and fun at the same time, which I liked as a concept. "*Buka u modi*" (Noise in Fashion) was blaring from my stereo. I was in tenth grade and it seemed as if the opportunities before me were unlimited.

Trotoar (Pavement), the local magazine dedicated to the alternative scene, appeared at the right moment, just when Ace of Base's "All That She Wants" or Snow's "Informer" were daily assaulting our ears. We could finally learn more about our idols at a time when we didn't have the internet and things weren't just a mouse click away. We had to order books from overseas and go to the university library to copy out texts by hand or photocopy them, but we didn't mind because we were hungry to know more.

Heavy metal was evolving. After the death of Metallica there weren't many bands left that could blow us away, with the exception of Sepultura, who continued to sing about socially relevant topics on their album *Territory*, something quite uncommon for a metal band. Meanwhile, in the former Yugoslavia fierce territorial battles were being fought. In the old days people used to ask, "Who are you? Where are you from?" with an interest and desire to get along with you. Now the standard reply was just, "I'm a nonentity."

The guitar on U2's "Numb" roared, catching the world unprepared. Music became a thumping heartbeat, a machine propeller, a car engine . . . I listened to it and thought about "my" Einstürzende Neubauten, who'd been making music like that for years . . . It seemed that pop-rock music was evolving and catching up with rap, which was always experimenting. *Insane in the Brain* by the timeless Cypress Hill and *Bacdafucup* by the short-lived Onyx breathed new life into the scene, while Body Count blended metal with rap in a completely new way that I liked. Headbanging to rap was a challenging concept. My heavy metal friends teased me for doing it, but hey, that's a completely different story.

This is the story in which tennis star Monica Seles was attacked with a knife, after which her career would never be the same, while her attacker received only a light sentence. But that was just another one of the many injustices of 1993 to which the world turned a blind eye. Another reason for people to keep their heads down and retreat inside themselves.

"Sober" by Tool was playing on MTV. I wondered to myself, "Are we all just puppets trapped in the containers we put ourselves in?" It seemed as if the whole country was stuck in a world of its own. Spurned by others, we fought hard to survive, but the fight was wearing us down. And as if that wasn't enough, the period of economic transition then finished us off. People were losing their jobs right and left. And songs like Björk's "Human Behavior" and albums like Dead Can Dance's *Into the Labyrinth* seemed like soundtracks that perfectly matched that kind of atmosphere. We had entered the labyrinth of transition, from which there has yet to be any escape.

▶▶ 1994 ◀◀

"Smells Like Teen Spirit"—Nirvana*

APRIL 6, 1994. Two years since the start of the bloody war in Bosnia. Like every spring for the next twenty years, we welcomed nature's reawakening and the sun's warm rays not with joy, but with fear. Would we be next? Would we dodge the bullets for another year? And then it happened.

The gun went off, aimed not at our heads, but at the lead singer of the most popular rock band of the '90s—Nirvana.

Once again, by some unknown force, my youth had been torn apart. My hopes for a better world—one in which art and music would be valued more highly than killing and prejudice—were dashed. It was a time of tumultuous events that changed me as a person and that made me angry and rebellious. But at the same time it made me apathetic, it gave me the constant feeling that I was incapable of doing anything, that I was the plaything of greater forces, swept along like a log down a river. And I felt that all I could do was capitulate. I threw my hands up and let the current take me wherever it wanted. What the hell!

We were teenagers with long messy hair, ripped jeans, and colorful T-shirts at a time when they were pretty much frowned upon. If you were late to class and wore a DIY T-shirt, it meant you were automatically in trouble and no excuse was going to

---

* "Smells Like Teen Spirit" dates from 1991, but is listed here in the context of the death of Kurt Cobain.

save you. Back then you were judged by your appearance and you had to work really hard to gain the teacher's respect, whereas today you can dye your hair green, have tattoos, and at the same time be into turbo-folk, and the teacher will be powerless to do anything about it. But this is only the tip of the iceberg when it comes to the problems we now face. The fact that today ripped jeans are sold in designer stores instead of kids buying normal jeans and sandpapering them and ripping them with their own scissors and is also not a major problem. It's just a symptom of it.

Kurt Cobain died. In fact, he killed himself. Some kids organized a memorial out front of the main Cathedral in Skopje. They chose the Cathedral not out of a naïve sense that someone who'd corrupted all the youth, glorified drugs, sex, and punk rock, and ended up killing himself should be paid religious tribute, but because at the time it was where all the alternative-minded young people gathered at night to consume large quantities of beverages. Beverages that had been produced by the religious orders in the monasteries for centuries.

I was sitting on one of the benches with my best friend, Vlad. We were young, physically and mentally immature, confused, filled with frustration, but we thought "we knew it all" and that we had the right to our own opinion on everything. Vlad was a metalhead at heart who saw alternative people as poseurs. He'd often tease me with the song *"Lažen alternativec"* (Fake Alternative) from a demo cassette by the then-young hip-hop band SAF. In the '80s, it was well known that metalheads and rappers couldn't stand each other. And besides, the fact that he could use a rap song mocking alternative people to have a dig at me was to him like killing two birds with one stone.

The song *"Keljav Dabar"* (Bald Beaver) by hip-hop band Čista Okolina featuring alternative rock band Last Expedition, which we both liked, muddied the waters even more. True, I was alternative and, true, metalheads didn't like rappers, but equally they hated punks, not to mention New Romantics. Everyone hated them. But often some metalhead would get involved with some New Romantic chick. And then everybody made fun of him. But the New Romantic chick would quickly turn into a metalhead, never the other way around. Many young people go through phases, but no one was a metalhead just for "one summer." "Metal for life" is not just a random expression.

Unlike my classmates, my favorite place to go to after school wasn't Aero, where they all met to have a drink and a chat. Solitude was my friend. And the prophetic words "books are my best friends," which I heard a girl from my neighborhood say in 1986, and which had made me laugh out loud, now seemed like the definition of my life.

I found peace over the Stone Bridge at the Kultura Bookstore. I'd been going there for years; I spent whole afternoons there after school. But when the Tabernacle Bookstore opened at the Macedonian National Theatre, the classics were eclipsed by modern literature. The literature I found at Tabernacle "sort of splattered my head all over the walls," to borrow the words of William Gibson on his first experience of reading William Burroughs. It was there I first discovered both Gibson and Burroughs, and it was there I found the most important source of alternative culture and art in my life: *Margina*. A local magazine with articles on virtual intelligence, cyberpunk, experimental literature, and many other esoteric ideas. Ideas that made me fantasize about and yearn for a different kind of reality than our own stale and stagnant turbo-folk.

My hands shaking, I handed the second issue of *Margina* to the man behind the counter, the excitement building inside me. I ran home, clutching the magazine tightly in its wrapper, looking around me sheepishly as though I were carrying a dirty magazine. That walk home seemed like the longest thirty minutes of my life.

I finally reached my house, threw down my rucksack, and started reading. At that moment, my life changed forever.

"Iron Maiden are losers, bro. They used to say that synthesizers have no place in heavy metal, but then they started using them too," I teased Vlad. I couldn't just let him take the piss out of me. What synthesizers were in the '80s became electronic music in the '90s, which was deeply embedded in all spheres of music, including heavy metal. The mixing of genres was no accident, but Vlad was a purist, whereas I was promiscuous—each of us music fanatics in his own way.

I sang a line from Beck's song "Loser." Vlad just rolled his eyes. That's how the round of adolescent teasing and mutual ridicule usually ended. Until the next time, that is.

"I'd kill for a cigarette right now," I said. We rarely smoked—"only at parties" as Vlad once stated in response to the doctor's query about his inflamed throat at a school medical check-up. Legendary.

"Me too, but it's daytime," he gave me a look as if to say he didn't want to risk getting caught. In any case, we didn't have any cigarettes. The conversation, like our little gathering, was pointless.

Most of the people there weren't even fans of Nirvana. The raw, unpolished sound of *Bleach* didn't change their lives. Their minds weren't "transported" by "Blew." "Love Buzz" made no impression on them. Even *Nevermind* didn't make their jaws drop. They'd come because it was trendy. There were also those who were there only to tease the "fake alternatives." Kečer showed up and greeted me with a loud: "One less redneck in the world!"

I smiled and greeted him with a wave. It's true that punks hated alternative people too, but their coming together like that was a mutual admission that something monumental was happening in music, something that woke us all up, made us snap out of a lot of things, forced us out of the house.

It was April 9, 1994. Saturday. A sunny day with no signs of thunderstorms. But in the Balkans, you can never be sure.

▶▶ 1995 ◀◀

"Hell is Round the Corner"—Tricky

THE PRODIGY WAS one of the bands Vlad used to tease me about. I was so obsessed with their song "Out of Space" that it was as if some sort of cosmic electromagnetic radiation had seeped into my brain and altered its molecular structure. I started looking at music differently. My interest in electronic music taught me that your attitude to art could be emotional and charged, as well as considered and intelligent. And it was here, too, that the roots of my future obsession with drum 'n' bass were born.

But the time wasn't ripe for that style of music. Macedonia was still hung up on the old folk tunes, like *Teškoto*.[2] We were progressing slowly, feeling self-conscious about not keeping up with modern trends and the progress of the world, when all of a sudden, something I could never have dreamed of happened: The Prodigy came to Skopje!

They exploded onto the stage with "Their Law" and the crowd went wild. I threw myself into the mosh pit. I was an old hand at slam dancing, shaking my head, screaming wildly, and occasionally hitting other people. But the crowd bore me off. Along the way, I was kicked and punched several times. While reeling from the blows, I realized that the time of slam dancing

---

[2] "The Hard One," a traditional folk song that speaks of hardship and struggle, devoted to Macedonians sending off loved ones starting their journey to an unknown hard life abroad. — *Translator's note*

was over, and that kicking and punching for fun had taken over instead. Then the war in Bosnia ended.

I was studying for a math exam. It was winter. Something about the warmth inside the house, along with the sound of "Protection" by Massive Attack featuring Everything But the Girl playing in the background, made the pile of practice tests lying next to me seem less terrifying. Besides, I believed in hard work and effort.

The West had finally come to Bosnia's aid. The Dayton Agreement was signed. My former country was split up and its people were left decimated, demoralized, scattered all over the world. Only a few of the old "Sarajevans" stayed on. Lots of new-comers moved in; unfamiliar people arrived and imposed their own ways. What little remained of the old Sarajevan spirit was now gone. But realistically, what else could one expect in such a situation? People who had been at the mercy of others were just glad the hell was over. Now what was needed was for the mess to be cleaned up and for people to look to the future.

I was a guy who was in love with the "wrong kind of girl," who read the "wrong kind of books," who liked the "wrong kind of movies," and listened to the "wrong kind of music." And then trip-hop music entered my life in a big way. Like a soundtrack recorded for alienated individuals living in fast times, where everything seemed to be changing at breakneck speed. "Hell Is Round the Corner" meant something completely different, but to me "hell" meant the despair of not having "her". Classic teen behavior.

My sister was working on the cover design of issue No. 13-14 of the art and culture magazine *Margina*. An issue that became famous because it had a hole in the cover and below it the letters VR for Virtual Reality on a mirrored surface, like Alice's mirror world in *Alice's Adventures in Wonderland*. The internet stormed into our lives at a time when we weren't used to having easy access to things.

Everything we'd worked for, everything we'd achieved in our country we had earned with blood, sweat, and tears. Then all of a sudden, the electronic highways were upon us. Vilém Flusser was talking about the information superhighway, whose lanes were being built with unprecedented speed. We had only just started to learn how to surf these lightning-fast superhighways, non-stop, without hesitation, and full of the desire to know more.

Portishead's "Mysterons" was playing on my stereo. "Is it hip-hop, dub, electronica, ambient music, or what?" I wondered. I didn't know the answer. But I knew that I liked it. Downtempo vibes at home.

Up-tempo riffs at Hotel Sileks in Ohrid.

"Who are this band?" Vlad asked.

"They sound a bit like the Beastie Boys, those guys who sang 'Fight For Your Right (To Party!)' from the eighties, don't they?" I said in an excited rush, which made him laugh. But then "Sabotage" was a bit different. Vlad seemed to like the song anyway. I don't know if it was because the name of the song was the same as the title of a Black Sabbath album or because of their guitar sound.

"Sabotage" boomed from the cassette player. Vlad and I were slamming against each other, while our classmates backed away from us. I didn't care—I was in the moment and enjoying the perfect blend of my two favorite musical styles. The Beastie Boys were hardcore punk rockers before they became rappers, and there you have it, the reconciliation of two seemingly quite different worlds. "There's still a chance for peace in the world," it seemed to me.

The world around me was spinning and I fell down on the ground hard. I was thrown in the shower to sober up. In my first drunken teenage madness, I came out stark naked, looking for clean clothes in a room filled with people. Ah, youth!

Our teenage years were slowly coming to an end and we were getting ready for more serious things. Only one more year and . . .

►►1996◄◄

"Ratamahatta"—Sepultura

I RANG THE DOORBELL of the fifth-floor apartment of an old building built during the socialist era in the neighborhood of Skopje known as Karpoš. Vlado came out. I waved a cassette in front of him.

"Mm-hmm," he said, half-asleep. That was his usual response to everything. We used to tease him, saying a dog was man's best friend whereas his was his bed.

"Have a listen to this." I pushed past him and entered the kitchen-cum-dining room-cum-living room. I extracted the Led Zeppelin cassette from his little cassette player and inserted my own cassette. After the soothing sound of Indian chants and the mesmerizing percussion suggestive of an ethno album, Max Cavalera's voice erupted and the roar of the guitar shook Vlado to the bones, taking his breath away and putting an abrupt end to his afternoon nap.

"What's this?" he asked excitedly.

"The new Sepultura album. Listen to the sound!" It was a new experience for me. The eclectic '90s had once again proven to be brave and inventive.

Music Garden was a place where we could slam dance to Sepultura's "Ratamahatta" without getting our ribs broken or our heads split open. It was an outdoor venue located between the Marakana live music club and the mini-golf course at the amusement park. Near the Army stadium. They played rock and alternative music at Music Garden. My friend Vlado referred to it mistakenly as "Soundgarden." He would often mix up names. Like in the Florida Deli at the Bunjakovec Market, where instead of asking for some *bukovec* (cayenne pepper) on his sandwich, he'd ask for some *bunjakovec*. That legendary sandwich filled with five smelly kebabs, a toxic dose of onions, and greasy fries on top. But it cost only 35 denar, which for us was affordable on our virtually non-existent budget.

It was the final year of high school. Once again, I had fallen in love with "the wrong girl." She liked the hit song "Children" by Robert Miles. Every time I heard the song, I thought of her. My taste in music went out the window. But if anything good came of that song it was the fact that it revived my interest in electronic music.

Music Garden was a true musical Garden of Eden, and we were its young and innocent denizens. The cops would come around almost every other night and turn off the music just as things were really getting started. The reason was that it was late, the music was too loud, and it was "bothering" all the homeless people trying to get to sleep on the park benches not far away. Yet, just fifty yards away, turbo-folk songs blared from a disco at the amusement park. But the dudes in tight black T-shirts and pointy shoes at that venue weren't breaking the law. No, they were (and still are) above it, because when the reedy sound of an accordion rings out and a voice virbrates with a certain "folk frequency," the laws relating to loud music are bent to accommodate them.

Ever since Music Garden closed down, Skopje's never really had another venue like it—a space where young alternative people can regularly gather in large numbers. What happened to it was in tune with the times. Dark forces were working to destroy the alternative art and culture scene. People were powerless to stop it. Least of all the apathetic youth of the '90s. They were disillusioned by the wearisome years when Macedonia was transitioning from being a socialist to a capitalist country, and by the wars, the absence of any real choice, the lack of any real future.

Goldie's seminal album *Timeless* catapulted him and drum 'n' bass to mainstream success. We might not have known what an "Amen Break" was, but we knew that we desperately liked that sound, a legacy of the breakbeat and big beat sound of The Prodigy.

Then a venue called Menada opened up and the D 'n' B parties began. Dancing to this type of music was hard work if you tried to follow the rhythm, because you could be mistaken for having an epileptic fit. The trick was to step to every second or fourth beat as if, let's say, you were dancing to a reggae beat.

But even more importantly, it was via those parties that the music of Roni Size came to Skopje. Many years later Roni himself came to Skopje. But by then, it wasn't that I was too old to experience his music in the same way, it was just that I wasn't young enough anymore. The new millennium had begun. Music and film seemed to be a dying art, symbolized by meaningless car chases, explosions, lack of plot, and cardboard cutout characters.

We went to a live gig at Zot, one of the last bastions of Skopje's underground music scene, with a toilet straight out of the film *Trainspotting*. Benzona was up first. Then Underdog came on. Vlad called them "Under a Dog." It was all mosh pits, binge drinking, and blurred perceptions through a haze of smoke and alcohol in a "basement atmosphere" where your id dominated your ego . . . Underdog were playing "Roxanne" by The Police. The crowd was going wild. We were packed in there like sardines. Behind us, some guys were playing table football and they were killing it.

In just under two years, a mind-altering revolution had happened in music. Grunge was at the peak of its popularity. Trip-hop legends Massive Attack, Portishead, and Tricky released groundbreaking albums. Then in September, I left to study in Italy. Those albums became the perfect soundtrack to my loneliness and alienation after I uprooted myself from the place I had only just begun to get used to. *Ciao Bella Macedonia!*

►► 1997 ◄◄

"The Box"—Orbital

A DISUSED FACTORY on the outskirts of Bologna. A sound system set up on the back of a truck and a DJ playing reggae music. I didn't recognize the band, but the atmosphere of peace and love appealed to me. I started dancing along with the crowd. We were united as one entity, one being. Someone grabbed me by the hand. I opened my eyes and dragged myself back to reality. An old man with a long, dirty, beard and torn clothes was smiling at me.

"He fancies you," my friend Alek called out, laughing wildly, clearly tripping on a psychoactive substance of some sort.

I jerked my hand away from the old man's grip. In the year and a half that I'd been studying in Italy, I needed some love and affection, but I wasn't looking for that kind of attention. I gave up on the reggae crowd.

The mystical sounds of "Nierika" by Dead Can Dance flowed through my headphones, creating a feeling of boundlessness around me. I didn't care where I was. I was drunk on music and alcohol. I rode my bike down the unfamiliar roads of Emilia-Romagna. I decided to keep riding and riding, without a destination. I left Cesena, the town where I was studying. The streetlights thinned out. There were cornfields all around, and the road gradually got rougher. I forgot about time and my own sense of loneliness. I forgot my nostalgia for Macedonia, the country that had taken me in and protected me, the place from which I had uprooted myself just as I'd started to settle down. My body was pedaling but my mind was far away, when all of a sudden—bang! I flew off the bike and slammed onto the asphalt with the full force of my drunken body. The music stopped.

Every part of me was in pain. But all I cared about was my Walkman. I'd bought it with my first scholarship payment—when it finally came through. For some reason, the money had been delayed. And because of that, I went hungry for months. I ate at homeless shelters. I ate the cheapest food in Italy—macaroni for lunch every day, and a glass of milk for dinner every night. Music was more important than pain, more important than having a full belly, more important than anything else . . . and in a flash it was gone. My Walkman was broken. I knelt on the asphalt in despair and broke into tears.

"Come on, hurry up," Alek yelled. He was right next to me, pacing back and forth like a madman in the railway parking lot.

"The chain won't budge," I said through gritted teeth. I heard a "clink" and the chain broke open.

"Come on, let's beat it!"

I hopped on the bike, and with the sound of The Chemical Brothers' "Block Rockin' Beats" in my ears, I pedaled as fast as I could. Adrenalin was pumping through us. We were young and irresponsible. Everybody stole bikes. I'd lost three of my own, and none of my friends had their own bike. It was part of student life in Italy. Like food vouchers or pot, everybody had done it once—the Rastafarian guy with dreadlocks from next door; the punk rocker from the soup kitchen who had a single braid trailing down his back with a bike bell at the end; the beautiful girl with glasses who got straight A's at university and who I really dug; and even my religious roommate, who'd pasted prayers from the Bible up on the walls of our room.

I had plastered my wall with posters of Jimi Hendrix, Nirvana, magnified microscopic bugs, galaxies, and electric guitars, framed by strips of multi-colored duct tape. They probably bothered my roommate, but he was too nice to say anything. He also never complained when I turned up the volume on Korn's A.D.I D.A.S." Amid all that mess stood four empty bread crates, two on each side, with a plank of wood on top. That was my desk. Beside my bed was an ashtray, overflowing with the remnants of hand-rolled cigarettes, because ordinary filter cigarettes were too expensive. Next to the ashtray was a radio cassette player. There was a program called "B Side" on Radio Deejay from Milan hosted by Alessio Bertallot and I used to tape the show on an audio cassette. That show kept me up to date with the latest developments in alternative music.

I was lying down on the lawn in front of the Malatesta Fortress, built in the fifteenth century by Malatesta Novello, a mercenary military commander from Cesena. I had read that the aristocratic Malatesta dynasty had gained their name because they were a bit "crazy in the head": *mala* meaning "bad" and *testa* meaning "head." I wasn't feeling good in the head at that moment either.

Unconsciously, I plucked a blade of grass. I pressed it against my chest, sobbing as I felt its pain. But the blade of grass calmed me. It told me that we were all just temporary in this world; we were all beings of energy that was converted from one form to another and that lived forever. Without end and without repose.

Twelve hours had elapsed since Blackie and I had smoked a joint, and my high still hadn't subsided. "Something's not right with me," I thought to myself, scared to death by the idea that I would never rid myself of that state. My mind was racing with chaotic thoughts. I understood the gist of my thought process, and at the same time everything seemed pointless to me. It took several more days for reality to return.

Cannabis sensitivity—was it intolerance or just inexperience? I'll never know because I never bothered to try it again.

House music was playing in one of the rooms at the disused factory. I steered clear of it. In another part of the factory, they were playing drum and bass. "Ain't Talkin' 'bout Dub" by Apollo 440 was taking me places. I looked around for Alek. I found him in front of the comics bookstore set up in one of the factory sheds. He was with a friend. The guy was shaking from laughing so hard, he fell to the ground. I ran over to help.

"Leave him. He's on LSD," Alek said. His friend's eyes looked right through me and I walked off in fright.

All night I could hear drums playing. I followed the sound. A crowd of people were sitting around, encircling a fire like a big snake. Lots of large pipes with smoke coming out of them were being passed around from person to person. I could swear I heard the sound of a didgeridoo. Alek laughed and told me they were bongs for smoking dope. I took off.

I walked through Piazza Maggiore, the main square in front of San Petronio Basilica. It was built in the sixteenth-century, and according to its original plans it was supposed to be bigger than St. Peter's Basilica in Rome. But the Pope wouldn't allow it.

"Marijuana—*si*. Eroina—*no!*" said a large banner in front of an abandoned building on the outskirts of Bologna. Students were squatting there. They cooked and ate together out in the yard, and lived, studied and slept together inside. There were different things going on all around—different kinds of music playing and different kinds of art being made in every room. Just like at the disused factory. "Killing in the Name" by RATM was blaring in the big entrance hall. I started slam dancing—on my own!

Outside, an Italian girl offered me a ride home. It was two in the morning. I left my bike—let someone else have it. She had seen me dancing and had taken a fancy to me. I marveled at her courage.

And then I lost my scholarship to study in Italy. I was disappointed and lonely. The call to adventure heralded by Daft Punk's "Around the World" turned into "The Box" by Orbital. Infinite solitude amid limitless possibilities.

I promised the Italian girl I would come back to Italy. I didn't know that I was telling her a lie.

▶▶ 1998 ◀◀

"The Dope Show"—Marilyn Manson (1998)

ON THE WAY back home from Italy to Macedonia, we stopped
off in Budapest to visit a friend of Alek's. We were listening to
Rabih Abou-Khalil's album *Arabian Waltz* and having a heavy
conversation about the universe, politics, and the future of the
Balkans. We took a walk around the city that night. People were
ice-skating on the frozen lakes. We then found a warm, cozy
place where we ate sliced bread fried in lard and topped with
fried onions, all washed down with beer. Contemporary pop
music was being played in the upstairs area, but we stayed down-
stairs to listen to the musicians playing traditional violin music.
They sat down at our table and the sound of Hungarian violins
filled us with melancholy and a sense of epic tragedy.

"*Sör . . . Sör!*" one of the violin players called out, wiping the
sweat from his brow. Even though we didn't understand what
he was saying, his hand gestures told us that they wanted some
beer. We ordered four Arany Ászoks—"working-class beers"—
and drank while those Hungarian violins tore at our souls.

I was back home in Skopje. I felt as if I'd wasted the chance
to make something of my life, but at the same time I was glad to
be home. If I belonged anywhere at all—it was here. We started
going to SF, a small venue, but still underground enough to
make up for Skopje's otherwise scant alternative scene.

Korn's "Freak on a Leash" came on. I started slam dancing

in an area about ten feet wide, skillfully avoiding the mirrors around me and the sharp-edged tables that were begging for an accident. Now, I won't say that a girl noticed me here too and that because of her I started listening to The Gathering, Tiamat, Moonspell, Anathema, and other goth metal bands, because that didn't happen. Just as I didn't slam into any windows or split my head open believing there was another room behind the mirror. No, behind every mirror is a parallel universe and that's why I didn't smack into the mirror, but rather passed through it and found myself in an entirely different reality.

I enrolled as a first-year medical student. Back then, I thought that maybe every student should first try studying medicine for a month. If they survived, then any college course after that would seem easy.

Let's just say that the first fifty pages of my medical textbook, describing the radius and ulna bones, filled with Latin terms and the names of every cavity, protuberance, or hole for a blood vessel or nerve, which had to be learned in a week, was something that didn't exactly sit well with Faith No More's "We Care A Lot".

Faith No More sang about disasters, fires, floods, starvation, and other human catastrophes, a dirty job but someone had to do it. But who cared about the outbreak of the Kosovo war when the Winter Olympic Games in Japan were in full swing? Who would care about the four million victims of the Congolese war over the next five years when the world was fixated on Posh Spice's wedding ring and her upcoming marriage to the guy with the best haircut in the history of soccer, David Beckham? Who cared about the disarmament crisis in Iraq that would lead to a war based on lies when millions of people around the world were distracted by Monica Lewinsky's allegations?

It was 1998. The colorful Windows 98 logo glowed on our home computers—at least for those who were debt free and could afford a computer. For those who had paid employment instead of foreign currency accounts that were blocked anyway. Or for those who'd retained their moral values instead of worthless stocks from failed enterprises that only a decade ago were promising to pay out dividends for a blue-chip retirement.

That year NASA's Galileo spacecraft detected water on Jupiter's moon Europa. This provided new hope for future generations that would seek a better future far away from their native planet.

Of course, Europe was as distant to us as the Moon—and still is, believe it or not! But none of that was of any concern to me. And the fact that France won the World Cup didn't interest me in the slightest either. I was having my own personal struggle with a college course I didn't like, for a better future I didn't want.

I desperately wanted to write and I spent whole nights in search of just the right words to put down on paper. I wanted to hand-paint T-shirts. I wanted to read books, watch films, listen to music. None of this fit in with dissecting dead lab rats at seven in the morning in sub-zero temperatures while the fog outside still blanketed the city. That kind of "dope show"—like something out of a Marilyn Manson clip—was just not my thing.

Let's get one thing perfectly straight: it's rare for anyone to study medicine because they love science. Most do it for the status and position. It allows them to go to the front of the line in banks or government services, and later in life it means they can avoid waiting for medical or specialist care for their kids. I'm not trying to condemn or justify anyone's actions, because I've had need of medical and specialist care in the past too.

"Let him through, he's one of us." They let me jump the line. As I passed the people waiting their turn to get an X-ray, I had the feeling that I was treading on their heads. With my head down, out of the corner of my eye I noticed a woman with "things" that no longer looked like legs, but more like hunks of shriveled meat skewered with iron rods. I felt ashamed of myself, but I walked past her and went in anyway.

Jamiroquai's "Deeper Underground" was a hit that year. I was withdrawing deeper and deeper inside myself—to the point of self-destruction. It was as though I wanted to confirm what my dad, the doctor in our family, thought of me: that I wasn't a worthwhile human being, that he'd been right to reject me, and that I deserved whatever I got or lost in life—of course, I was just looking for excuses to be frivolous and immature.

Lauryn Hill's amazing video for "Everything is Everything" was playing on TV. And I really did believe that everything was possible and that everything was true, that there were no lies because there were endless possibilities for a given reality to become true—one in which we are all both perpetrators and victims, winners and losers. I recognized those aspects of myself, but I still wasn't sure what to do with them.

Trip hop made a comeback with albums by Massive Attack and Tricky. But it was short-lived—the music was too slow and out of step with the fast-paced digital age in which Google was founded. The term "Google it" dominated the virtual world of information, synonymous for knowledge and power.

Hugo Chávez was elected President of Venezuela and he would bravely defy a world power, while our country, Macedonia, was still trying to please those more powerful than itself. Lacking initiative, determination, and with no real sense of what real freedom is, we were just stuck in our own inertia. We didn't know where we were going or even whether there was anywhere to go.

We added a leap second at the end of the year . . . Or maybe we lost a second of our lives before setting foot in the New Year, which was not a good omen.

▶▶ 1999 ◀◀

"Walk This Land"—E-Z Rollers

THE KOSOVO WAR escalated and NATO intervened. I gave up college again, and went to a more peaceful part of the world to try to make sense of it all.

"Do you like drum 'n' bass?" I asked the head cook, a young guy from Wales with a wicked cooking technique, like something out of a movie—tossing vegetables high into the air in a wok, flambéing the food and dousing it with broth that dripped off the edge of the wok and sizzled on the burner. And all to the sounds of Micky Finn & Aphrodite blaring from a cassette player beside him.

"Course I do, mate! D'you like it? Who're your favorite bands?"

"Yeah, I do ... Alex Reece, Goldie, Roni Size & Reprazent . . ." I rattled off the most famous names as if from an encyclopedia. He added, "Alex Reece—he's great, mate. And 'Candles'—that's a great track!" Then he asked me about Macedonia and the conflict in Kosovo.

"The Albanians really don't like the Serbs, but they don't mind the Macedonians," a young girl cut in. She had fled civil war from somewhere in Africa. I confirmed what she said and told them that it was a bit different in our country. We weren't as chummy with each other as we'd once been in the former Yugoslavia, but we didn't hate each other either.

75

The head cook rolled a joint, licked the edge to seal it, and then lit up, inhaling deeply. He coughed, and then, as though a thought had suddenly popped into his head, he raised his arms in the air. "Your people dance like this, don't they?" he asked, skillfully imitating a ring dance. I laughed and nodded. He then prepared a quick tasty chicken, rice, and vegetable dish that we ate with chopsticks.

The boss couldn't stand me. He always looked at me with suspicion, as if I'd come from some godforsaken land to take the bread out of his mouth or steal something from his Asian-inspired restaurant. Yet I worked hard. Even the jungle DnB dude vouched for me, telling him I was a "good worker." But the boss wasn't prepared to acknowledge it, not even when I worked two shifts—fourteen hours washing dirty dishes with the remnants of meals that cost as much as I earned in three days. As if I wasn't worth the little money I was being paid.

"First you throw the leftovers in the trash, then you rinse the dishes and put them into the dishwasher." He opened the huge industrial dishwasher and hot steam rose in the air. "But before that, you take out the washed dishes, making sure to protect your hands from the steam when you open it, and you stack them on the shelves. It's simple. And don't take too long because the whole chain in the kitchen will be disrupted."

Real simple. The first night the dirty dishes piled up so high that everybody started complaining. Even though the DnB dude was helping me, I couldn't remember where to put all the dishes and pots in the overcrowded kitchen. In a rush, I broke a plate and because I'd been told the cost of every broken dish would be deducted out of my pay, I secretly threw it in the trash. But all in all, with the sound of "Walk This Land" by E-Z Rollers in the background, it wasn't so bad.

Later that night, after I cleaned the kitchen and the toilet, I took out the garbage. As I was dragging the bag up the steps, the broken plate tore the bag open and all the food spilled out across the stairs. Even more farcical was that there were metal grates on the concrete steps. I had to clean them one by one to make sure I'd removed all the leftovers, otherwise my pay would be docked.

A group of guys were hanging out in front of the closed restaurant. Like in some American gang film. I didn't have the guts to walk past them. I waited for them to leave before showing my face outside. I went out onto Portobello Road, which had been made popular because of that soppy movie, *Notting Hill*. But the place still buzzed with dodgy types and it was a true reflection of cosmopolitan London, where you could bump into anyone from a Jamaican to someone from the Balkans. But in the end a job was a job. No one made me take it. I made more money there in a week as a dishwasher than I did in a whole year back home working as a freelance writer and translator, so it was worth it.

The cousin who used to switch off my Guns 'n' Roses tape back in 1985 would have been proud of me. I'd started listening to Idoli, Haustor, Šarlo Akrobata, and Azra. I was a late starter when it came to Yugoslav alternative and new wave music from the '80s. But my country, which was in a jam due to problems with its neighbors, was drawing me in once again.

Vlado and I went camping at Lagadin, a small tourist village on the banks of Lake Ohrid. We were both twenty-one and had recently broken up with our girlfriends. We brought along an old, battered cassette player that lent an added charm to the already poor-quality cassettes we played on it. I'd moved on from my love of crackly hi-fidelity LPs to almost unrecognizable punk, hardcore or metal recordings. We cleaned the scratched and dirty cassette heads with alcohol. We spliced and rewound the broken ends of tape that tore from being played endlessly. All of this was in keeping with the DIY ethos or the punk ethics of "do it yourself."

We'd set up camp near the campground entrance. People kept looking to see who those "filthy, noisy metalheads" were, as they could hear the music blaring from our beat-up cassette player. Their looks and stares offended me as much as our music or style of dress provoked them.

But in a weird way I liked it. I've always wanted to be disapproved of, to be different from everyone else. Maybe because that's how I justified my own meaning and existence.

At the time I thought, "to be different is to exist." But I didn't realize that I was actually seeking confirmation of my individuality from precisely the people that I wanted to distinguish myself from. That was the paradox of my life.

We listened to The Gathering day and night, especially their *Mandylion* album, in which menacing tones and heavy guitar riffs are juxtaposed with the singer's ethereal vocals. The music seemed to illuminate an unseen part of my soul, while the sky above us—normally shrouded in Skopje smog—revealed thousands of previously unseen celestial bodies.

Right then I felt the urge to write a kids' book on astronomy, because they didn't teach us about science in ordinary life, especially about things to do with the universe. In the Balkans people are quick to judge each other and then refuse to try to understand each other. We needed things to help us develop a broader and more open perspective on things.

My own perspective on music was regressing. It seemed as though I was looking back instead of looking forward. But the war in Kosovo ended, and that was a good thing.

More peaceful times lay ahead . . . or so it seemed.

▶▶ 2000 ◀◀

"The Time is Now"—Moloko

3, 2, 1 . . . HAPPY NEW YEAR! And then . . . silence. Nothing happened. The "Millennium bug" didn't bite us and people breathed a huge sigh of relief. People then carried on creating concrete jungles, poisoning and polluting the planet, cutting down forests, and mining precious metals that made some people rich while harming everybody else. It was business as usual that summer in the Year of Our Lord, 2000.

But for me, more important was another centenary: the one-hundredth anniversary of the publication of *The Interpretation of Dreams* by Sigmund Freud, the founder of psychoanalysis. The perfect time for self-examination. I regularly wrote down my dreams and I started having psychoanalysis sessions with a neuropsychiatrist, Dr. Marina, our country's only expert in Jungian analytical psychology.

"I dreamed of my dad's name written in graffiti. I took out a gun and fired shots at it," I told the doctor. My journey into the subconscious took hold of me. If there is a way to unlock the subconscious mind without drugs, then psychoanalysis is the key to it.

I enrolled to do Psychology. I passed all my exams on time. I did freelance translation. I wrote a lot, and was still sketching and drawing, and I had several things ready for publication. Had I finally found what I'd been looking for?

I also found my true love. We couldn't live without each other. When we were apart, we spoke for hours on the phone. We were so different and yet we fit together perfectly. Like yin and yang.

I was sitting on a concrete planter bench seat out the front of Zizi Top, one of the last bastions of the old rock 'n' roll sound in Skopje. She was with a girl I knew from high school. I immediately noticed her smile. Our first date was at a venue called New Age.

"One of the books will have an actual hole in the middle of it and the story will take place around that hole and interact with it." I was explaining my ideas about my books to her as she drew me in with her hazel eyes. And for the first time in my life, I just couldn't stop talking.

New Age no longer exists. At least not like it used to: the mystical ambience, the dim lights, the exotic teas, the warm wine, the *salep*, the coffee with Turkish delight—they're all gone. But the whispered chatting and the sound of Dead Can Dance remain. Zizi Top also no longer exists, but the concrete planter bench seat on which we spent our first night together, in endless conversation and furtive smiles, is still there as a reminder of former times. Music Garden was unfortunately closed down due to the combined forces of the police and turbo-folk set. But the live music played at Marakana and Lady Blue by the ever-present band Day Off more or less kept rock 'n' roll alive for us.

We both preferred small gigs to big concerts. In the past, we really enjoyed going to the Youth Cultural Center with its legendary café, and to the esoteric Kuršumli An, a restored caravanserai, with its New Age festivals and mythic concerts by Arhangel, Kismet, and Kiril. But then later on we felt more relaxed in smoky, intimate venues where the music filled the space with swelling sound that pulled you in and wouldn't let you go.

We fell in love with the Red Hot Chili Peppers album *Californication*—so much so that, years later, at our wedding reception, the first song we danced to was the last track, "Road Trippin'." That great album was a real trip for us.

"I couldn't get to sleep. I was constantly getting up and

writing something down: ideas, plans, concepts for stories . . . Sleep slowly overtook me, but then I started to suffocate and leaped out of bed. There was a pile of marbles in front of me, a huge cluster, enticing me to touch them. They were opaque, colorless. A few seconds later they just disappeared," I told Dr. Marina in her office, which coincidentally was located not far from New Age.

"They're nothing but hypnagogic hallucinations. They appear just before you fall asleep," she said. But I thought they were something more than that, some sort of message from my subconscious or superconscious that I was supposed to figure out.

Moloko's "The Time is Now" was playing through my headphones. I was typing like a madman on the outdated Pentium 1 with Windows 95 operating system that my sister had left me when she went to England. I wrote pages and pages of dreams, short stories, songs, and memories. All these, together with my five unpublished manuscripts, would be consigned to the past after I published my first book.

The walls in my basement room were covered with clippings from music and film magazines. There were ominous paintings by my favorite painters: Hieronymus Bosch, Edvard Munch, and Salvador Dalí, which created an atmosphere conducive to surfing the subconscious. I felt at ease in this underground world. That's where I used to get together with my friends. My basement room became like a hangout.

I wasn't aware of it at the time, but my girlfriend certainly wasn't very comfortable with my "underground" companions, people who lacked direction or purpose in life. They were usually the kids of divorced parents, people who'd experienced childhood trauma. Even though she liked rock and roll and went out to gigs, my girlfriend's life was orderly and focused. She had both her parents. She valued going to college and having a job. She'd been working and studying since she was twenty.

I needed her badly because she gave me a sense of normality. I admired her determination and perseverance. She made me feel grounded. She was my anchor in the chaotic storm of existence—something I'd been looking for my whole life.

We downloaded films and music and swapped them between ourselves. Even though the art and entertainment scene seemed to be in crisis that year, the old '90s always offered up something good. The fact that the century ended with cult films like *The Matrix, Fight Club, Dogma, Magnolia, Office Space, Lock, Stock and Two Smoking Barrels, Ghost Dog, Eyes Wide Shut, The Blair Witch Project*, and *American Beauty* perhaps suggested that people wanted to do their best before Y2K brought about Armageddon.

The Millennium bug terrified people across world. Nobody knew whether or not we'd go back to the pre-digital age. But now that everything has passed, people seem pretty relaxed. And with the exception of the movie *Snatch*, the art of popular film has given up good story telling at the expense of explosions, car chases, and cheap thrills.

"Each story is written down on a small sheet of paper measuring two by four inches. The physical limitation forces you to find and use only the right words . . ." I explained as I puffed on a West cigarette, holding the sheets of paper out in front of me. She looked at me with a sweet smile on her full lips. I was drunk on wine and on her, on the desire to write and create something never seen thitherto. The book with the hole and the micro stories were never published, like many of my other ideas. But that wasn't important. The important thing was that we were together and living in the moment.

We were celebrating New Year's at the Youth Cultural Center. The band Novogradska was playing. The new century had begun. We were young and full of life and plans for the future. We were burning with desires and dreams and we had great expectations. And then the future toyed with us once again.

►►2001◄◄

"Clint Eastwood"—Gorillaz

ONE MORNING SIMMERING ethnic conflict suddenly erupted into a serious armed conflict in Macedonia. Everything was uncertain. A feeling of insecurity hung over us like a thick fog. I was sitting my second-year psychology exams, while only ten miles away we could hear bombs exploding. As nature awoke from its long winter sleep, every day we were jolted awake by warplanes and our nerves were slowly worn down.

I was sitting with my aunt in her apartment in Sarajevo. I can remember I was watching a movie on TV, and she just kept talking and smoking one cigarette after another and putting them out in a jar half full of water. It was the first time in ten years that I'd been in her apartment, and I was struck by how everything looked exactly the same, as though it had been frozen in time. The cork coasters, the amber glass plates, the beige coffee cups—they were all still there where they'd always been.

My cousin's room still had the same wallpaper with the autumn landscape and the red lamp under which he would solve his calculus problems. Back then, the sine wave and the infinity symbols looked like weird alien hieroglyphs to me, like something straight out of *Arthur C. Clarke's Mysterious World*, which was actually lying on the shelf beside his stereo system. My cousin was forever playing *"Niko kao ja"* (No One Like Me) by Idoli on that stereo.

Bullet holes pocked the front wall of my aunt's apartment building, as well as the surrounding buildings, but there were no other visible signs of conflict inside the private world of her apartment. My uncle had stayed on in the apartment during the war in Bosnia. He was a reserved man, a physicist, with thick arms and a limpid look in his eyes. When I was a kid he used to play the card game Tablanet with me. He would do things like peel me an apple, cutting it into small slices that I ate with delight, and he would teach me the basics of physics, how gravity is defined, and ask me questions like, "How many legs does a horse have when it lifts one up?"

That question always reminded me of a scene from one of the cowboy comics my cousin kept in his closet, in which Lucky Luke lifts up the leg of his trusted horse and we can all see that it still has four legs. In 2001, "Clint Eastwood" by Gorillaz reminded us that we were living in times not unlike the Wild West, and the song introduced me to a world of new sound that really appealed to me.

My uncle was no longer alive. My aunt told me that he survived the war by sleeping in the hallway, away from the windows, that he helped all the neighbors and that they all respected him, even though he belonged to the "other" ethnicity and religion. And he was probably the only such man left in the whole building, probably even the whole neighborhood, my aunt said.

The TV program was suddenly interrupted by breaking news. I was in the middle of Sarajevo, a city that until five or six years ago had itself still been at war. But what I saw on TV absolutely stunned me. What followed was beyond all belief and I, my aunt, Sarajevo, Europe, and the world were numbed.

It was September 11, 2001 and the armed conflict in Macedonia subsided. A little less than a month earlier, an agreement was signed to ensure the rights of minorities. It seemed that better times were coming—at least for my country.

I'd been living in Belgrade for some time, planning to continue my psychology studies there. Meanwhile, my cousin took me to concerts and gigs by his band Vrooom and I explored the Serbian alternative music scene.

At night I hung around the 24-hour bookstores and got back late, drunk on the words and stories that lived within me. I read Daniil Kharms and it was like discovering the Holy Grail. I was given an old typewriter, and more out of devotion than necessity, I started writing short stories influenced by Kharms.

"Chop Suey!" by System Of A Down was listed as unsuitable for public broadcast in America, along with 165 other songs, many of which contained the word "fall," including every song by Rage Against the Machine. Alicia Keys's big hit "Fallin'," however, was not on that list—a testament to the hypocrisy of commemorating lives lost, but not at the cost of making money, which is still the main priority in the World Trade Center of life.

It was a time of pompous pronouncements and mobilization of the masses. Radiohead's "Pyramid Song" served as a counterpoint to the new era, which like a monster composed of fluorescent olive-green billboards hissed, roared, and spat out fire. The song invited introversion and introspection, while the piano accompaniment pounded out a historical truth, and the voice came from the depths of a severe depression, like the one that had engulfed our country.

That voice called out to us to give up, to surrender, to end the torment, while the violin enchanted like a Siren's song, romanticizing death. But faced with the prospect of mortality, no one awaits the end of their existence romantically; rather, they seek desperately to avoid it.

The dream continued and reality seethed with "Dream On" by Depeche Mode in the background. The *Tribute to Mizar* album was released to remind us of different times. I used to like Mizar's dark, goth, punk rock, ethno-ambient style. That year, 2001, their sound seemed to suit the times—a nationalistic, chest-beating call for war. I could no longer listen to them. Something inside me naturally railed against such ideas.

The Goth style began to seem Nazi-like, like kick in the back of the neck from a combat boot. Anathema's album *A Fine Day to Exit* rang the death knell for goth metal from my music box. Paradise Lost, My Dying Bride, Theatre of Tragedy, Moonspell,

Tiamat, and many other bands suddenly went out of my life, the same way they had entered it.

Daft Punk's "Harder, Better, Faster, Stronger" was there to cheer us up, to give us hope for a better, more modern Europe that didn't dwell on its own difficult past, but focused on the present and looked toward the future—for all its people . . . but what could music do when far greater, darker, forces ruled us, concerned only about that part of civilization to which we didn't belong. We were puppets to the whims of those more powerful.

Back home again. Back at New Age. The candle on the table flickered in front of us. Björk's "Pagan Poetry" playing in the background fit perfectly within the concept of an ethnically and religiously mixed society, like a potpourri of scents and sounds.

I was talking about books and music again, and underneath it I was utterly happy that my girlfriend and I had stuck together. She never gave up on me even when I took off out of the blue. But that was our Balkan reality—people live day by day without plans or future prospects, with their jaws set in a permanent scowl, their bodies rigid with cramp. We were primed to live a shared life like that forever.

▶▶ 2002 ◀◀

"By the Way"—Red Hot Chili Peppers

"Take off your glasses so I can see what you look like," said the man I'd called "Dad" more than ten years ago, the man who'd packed me into a car like a suitcase full of dirty laundry and left me at a railway station five hundred miles from home, to be handed in to Lost and Found. The owner of the suitcase was never found because there was no return address on the suitcase.

I found him in Montenegro, where he'd fled because of the war in Bosnia. He had a new wife and three new kids. I saw them sleeping on their little bunkbeds with the blankets falling off them, two boys in a bunk and a girl in a separate bed. Two little brothers and a sister who were strangers to me. I didn't even know their dad.

My girlfriend and I went to Belgrade intending to look for him, but with no real plan. I got in touch with some old acquaintances who put me in contact with some other people and, somehow, I traced him to Podgorica in Montenegro. Then we went on holiday to Herceg Novi, on the Montenegrin coast, and met him there.

My dad achieved something that even the war had never succeeded in doing—I dropped out of college in a desperate, masochistic attempt to confirm his demoralizing words: "You're a rotten apple, just like your mother."

I got drunk on the electro-rock sounds of the Darkwood Dub

album, and took comfort in the message of its title: *Život počinje u 30-oj* (Life Begins in Your 30s). Maybe there was still hope for me. I closed the door to my room. I closed all the windows. And I closed myself off. The only thing left open was the MS Word file on my computer. I filled the blank pages on the screen with words as if my life depended on it, every night from midnight to 6 a.m. I waited for my mom to get up to go to work before I went to bed. Sometimes I skipped a whole night's sleep. I lived in a world that no longer resembled reality. But something good came out of it: my first book.

"God, it's suffocating in here!" Vlado entered my room and opened all the windows and shutters. I imagined myself crawling into a corner of the room and screeching like a bat. The ashtray on my desk was overflowing with cigarette butts, the twenty I'd smoked that night. Johnny Cash's cover of "Hurt" by Nine Inch Nails, which had been on repeat the whole night, was playing through the computer speakers. Vlado changed the song, but I didn't ask him why. I myself knew how depressing it was.

"I had to rewrite a short story. I accidentally closed it without saving it. It took me the whole night . . . I just had to rewrite it, but the second version is different," I groaned. Vlado just replied with his usual "mm-hmm."

The Red Hot Chili Peppers' "By the Way" was playing through the speakers. I turned up the volume full blast. A new day lay before me and I decided not to sleep it away.

I finished the book at the end of that year but I had no clear idea what to do with it. And then I woke up one morning feeling unprecedented determination.

"I dreamed I was sitting in the middle of the road writing. I pegged my stories up like clothes on a line. Passers-by could read and buy the stories. When I woke up I knew I had to find a publisher for the book," I told Dr. Marina.

I met up with Koljač—"the butcher"—the editor of a magazine that had changed my entire outlook on life almost ten years ago. People could say whatever they wanted about my work. I really didn't care because I knew what I was doing. But my confidence in myself was once again tested.

"The whole thing has to be rewritten. And what's this non-sense—why does the story end this way? It doesn't make sense. You have to cut this completely . . ." Koljač didn't mince words. The manuscript I had printed out with a cover, just like a real book, was soon filled with his comments and scribbles. I feigned understanding and indifference. My heart was beating like mad.

"But it's good. I like it. We'll publish it," he said in what I came to learn was his usual style: if he liked something, at first he'd ruthlessly criticize it and then conclude that he liked it. I still left there though with mixed feelings and no clear idea of what to do next.

"It's Too Late" by The Streets, aka British white rapper Mike Skinner, was like a reflection of my own life. How many times had I arrived late to meet my girlfriend and how many times had I apologized to her, saying that I was writing and had lost all track of time. She knew I wasn't lying and would quickly forgive me. Then we'd go to Lady Blue—opposite the Army stadium, near the former Kultura cinema—one of our favorite venues, where the rock music filled the air with what felt like raw energy. Squeezed into that small, smoky place, we were drunk on love and music.

It was 2002 and Britney Spears was twenty years old. She was the most famous celebrity. I was twenty-five. "Dreaming" by Kismet was playing in the background, and I was thinking of giving up on everything. I couldn't write any more, let alone do another version of the book that I thought was already finished, without any need for revision. And I certainly couldn't stomach going to college again. I had no job, no prospects. And . . . where to from here?

►►2003◄◄

"Seven Nation Army"—The White Stripes (2003)

I STILL DIDN'T give up on my book. I ate, breathed, and lived that book. I cut a lot out and then rewrote the rest. In collaboration with Koljač, the final version was a minimalist product that invited the reader to explore the seeds that the book had planted. For the first time in my life I felt satisfied.

The first printed copy of the book arrived one morning. In fact, several copies. I didn't know how a first-time dad felt, but I was convinced it was exactly the way I felt then. I put on "Evolution Revolution Love," thrilled that Tricky had finally hit mainstream success, and leafed through my book. If happiness exists, then this is it, I thought to myself.

"So, you're not studying at college at the moment," the Army recruitment officer said. I said nothing. I just shook my head because I knew what was coming. I hadn't been to college in over a year. My book had been published and I had no new stories or ideas. I'd lost all interest in writing. It was as though I had poured everything into that book and now there was nothing left inside me. No ambitions or desires.

"Do you know how to cook?" the Army recruitment officer asked. That question seemed so absurd that I laughed out loud. "Well then, you'll work in the soldiers' mess," he said. Without a word I signed the form. I then gathered up my documents, and, driven by forces that were stronger than me and over which I had no control, as though in a Kafkaesque dream, I walked out and gave myself over to fate.

We got up at 4 a.m. every morning and tried in vain to keep warm in the van since the engine took a full half hour to warm up, after which it blew out hot air with the choking smell of diesel and burning rubber. The driver of the van was a cool guy who liked rock 'n' roll. Sometimes on the radio we'd catch "The Hardest Button to Button" by The White Stripes or "Seven Nation Army," a name oddly appropriate in our situation. We talked about the new wave of garage rock and what a much-needed boost it was to the bland music of the new millennium. Yes, the vitality and creativity of the '90s were needed now more than ever in the new century, which was satisfied just with recycling the music of previous decades. The other guy was a bit of a whack job with chipped and cracked teeth as if a firecracker had gone off in his face, cartoon-like ears, and a tall scrawny body. He never understood a word we were saying and was constantly laughing for no reason.

"My mom reckons she saw you checking out our car yesterday." I laughed and said nothing. That was "Bully Boy," who sometimes came in place of the whack job. He would threaten everyone and invent stories about how you stole something of his just to get into a fight with you.

"Great song," the older big guy, a Roma, said about OutKast's "Hey Ya!" blaring from the small radio in the kitchen. I was scrubbing pans with scraps of fried chicken. He pulled out a hidden box filled with leftover Eurocrem chocolate bars and Viva brand juice boxes. I knew he sold them at a street stall, but I didn't say anything to make him take offence. I never had any problems with the Roma. They were the ones who taught me that if you're smart it's best to play dumb so people leave you alone. All the Roma were smart, especially the other, chubby, young guy, who would bust into a breakdance without warning, and who deliberately wore a dumbfounded expression with the officers and constantly repeated to them, "I don't understand, sir."

We showered in the changing rooms at the Army stadium, near the amusement park, right next to the former Music

Garden, which made me feel nostalgic for the old venue. But you don't get much time for reflection in the army. The chubby Roma guy made us laugh with his dancing. "Look at this," he said and got down on the ground and did some moves, topping it off with a back spin. And buck naked too! Unreal.

We'd load up large containers of food weighing more than a hundred pounds into the van. Then we'd open the mess, arguing with the soldiers who always demanded more food and who accused us of stealing their meals. We'd wash the dishes and scrub the kitchen clean. We'd have an hour's rest and then the whole process would start over again. It was like that all day long, until night when we'd crash out in bed, only for the day to then just begin over again.

People stole all sorts of things from our room: shoes, pants, ties, belts . . . One of my buddies showed me how easy it was to pick a padlock. Once they even stole my toothbrush and toothpaste. But I could always leave a book on my pillow and still find it in the same place when I got back.

A corporal came in with a pile of sheets and threw them across one of the beds. Each of us grabbed one.

"Hey, these are soaking wet!" one of the younger soldiers protested.

"So?" was the corporal's cynical reply.

In the army you sleep on damp sheets and that's that, one of life's little facts you have to accept with dignity, while listening to Metallica's "St. Anger" through your headphones and wondering what's left of that favorite childhood band of yours.

I was assigned to coffee-making duties. In the breaks between making coffee and making the officers' beds, I had more time to read. Every morning we'd collect the officers' old newspapers and bring them the new ones. Reading the newspapers became my main way filling in time and I read them from the first page to the last.

Soon I began to notice similarities and patterns in the news stories. I imagined myself watching an insect-like creature with journalist tendencies knitting a web according to precise instructions encoded in its genetic program.

"Times Like These" by the Foo Fighters was playing on my Walkman. I was lying in a military hospital and I didn't know what to do with myself. The times were going nowhere for us. We still hadn't recovered from the unrest that still occasionally flared up. And then it hit me.

"I'll be a spider!" something inside me called out and I started writing my own newspapers—about the world as I saw it, isolated from the outside world. Out of the dystopia of the hospital and the barracks, I created my own utopia.

I had fun like never before. The band Mizar reunited and I was hoping for something new and exciting on the domestic music scene.

▶ ▶ 2004 ◀ ◀

"What You Waiting For?"—Gwen Stefani (2004)

EVERYDAY LIFE BROUGHT with it cruel awareness rather than joy. With no job and no prospects, I tried to put all the pieces of my broken past back together again. Instead of dealing with my problems, I decided to flee from them. But I didn't walk, I ran! Pushing aside anyone who stood in my way.

The music video for "Take Me Out" by Franz Ferdinand, with their socialist-realist allusions, was blaring from the TV. My girlfriend and I were having a fight. She left and "Let's Get It Started" by The Black-Eyed Peas came on, over-the-top and shameless, the perfect basis for a carefree life filled with superficial values. Music was definitely going through a crisis. Like me and my girlfriend.

Foltin's album *Donkey Hot* reminded us of the soundtrack to the movie *Amélie* and of a different time, when, surrounded by insecurity and fear, we used to cuddle up together and comfort each other.

That year saw the largest number of greatest hits albums in all of recorded history. It seemed as if music had exhausted itself. My studies seemed like an idea looming on the horizon, but so out of reach that they seemed unrealistic. And so far as work was concerned, I had no idea what to do.

"What You Waiting For?" by Gwen Stefani was playing on

the portable radio in my little red hatchback, a Yugo Koral 1.1i. Her song was the perfect description for my life back then.

"What are you waiting for, mate!" the driver behind me cried out, honking his horn for who knows how long. I was thinking about what lay ahead and whether we were ready for it. Our president had been killed in a plane crash and all of us were overcome by fear and uncertainty once again. America elected George Bush as their president. Evidence that water had once existed on Mars was discovered, while NATO continued its aggressive expansion into Eastern Europe. I pressed the pedal to the floor and set off into the unknown.

"I'm pregnant."

Some words can change your life. Suddenly all your problems are solved and you know what you have to do. Finally I had a purpose.

I submitted my manuscript of fabricated news stories, designed to look like a newspaper, to various publishers. But instead of getting my new book published, I got offered a permanent job as a book designer. Culture works in mysterious ways.

The sound of U2's "Vertigo" could be heard coming from the office of the former Točka Cultural Center. The center, located at 38 Ilindenska Boulevard, was a true center of alternative cultural life in Skopje, where many young artists began their careers.

I was working on the cover design of the *Margina* art and culture magazine, which had proved to be crucial to me several times in my life. A colleague with some literary pedigree and the habit of asking awkward and unexpected questions asked me about my writing experience.

"I'm not a writer. I just experiment with the written word," I replied. He wasn't satisfied with that. In the coming months, I would often come home shaking because of his biting comments. But even so, I still admired and respected him immensely, like all the others who worked there and who selflessly devoted themselves to building something more important than themselves. I became part of that whole community, but at the time I wasn't aware that it would become an integral part of my life forever.

I held my hand on B's stomach and spoke softly.

"Be good, my little munchkin." That's what I called my future child, even though it was then just a few cells that were developing with the speed of a cosmic miracle. And then I felt something I couldn't explain in words.

"What's wrong?" B asked.

"Nothing," I replied, and smiled because my child "told" me that my life would soon change and that I shouldn't worry, because from now on it would be the most important thing. It would no longer be about me or B, but about her, the tiny little girl who, from the moment she first looked at us from the incubator, became the center of our lives. And after her, her little brother too. But all that was yet to come and is a completely different story filled with new songs, new scenes, and new dreams.

The sound of the Red Hot Chili Peppers' "Road Trippin'" could be heard faintly in the distance.

The road was waiting for us!

CPSIA information can be obtained
at www.ICGtesting.com
Printed in the USA
FSHW012228200320

9 781628 973501